A Sister's Sanctuary

Brides of Mill Ridge

Book #6

CYNDI RAYE

A Sister's Sanctuary

Brides of Mill Ridge Series

Book #6
by
Cyndi Raye

Cover by silverheartstudio.com

---

1. http://www.CyndiRaye.com

Dedication

Thanks to all my readers who love to read these clean and wholesome books. I love having you all give me your opinion and put up reviews and if it weren't for you, then my work would mean nothing.
Thank you all from the bottom of my heart!

*****

Would you rather read the whole series in one shot?
Get Brides of Mill Ridge box set available on Amazon![1]
(https://www.amazon.com/gp/product/B07NKCHCTB)

---

1. https://www.amazon.com/gp/product/B07NKCHCTB

Chapter 1

Marlene heard a soft moo as the heavy-set, golden-brown cow made its way up the street at the exact same time two men turned to watch the action. She leaned front on the rocker, curious to what they were saying. "Fergenson's cow is loose again. Looks like Elda forgot it was Monday. Clarissa has laundry hanging on her head," the first man said.

The other fellow chuckled as they passed by Marlene's front porch. "Yep, she ought to know better. Every darn Monday and Thursday that cow has a hankerin' to take a long walk. She trudges right through Elda's laundry lines. Not even Fergenson can persuade her to go back home."

The man who spoke first shook his head. "Don't see what it matters any. Elda will be along any moment now, her loud obnoxious voice calling for the sheriff. I pay it no mind, after all, the cows minding its own business."

Marlene watched with amusement as the cow waddled its way down the middle of the street, a moo here and there. She stared at the bright yellow material wrapped around its brown neck.

"You bring back my curtain! Get back here you rotten thief!"

"I told you! Here she comes. The old batalak knows what days Clarissa takes her walk. Why does she bother doing laundry on those days?"

"Beats me. We best get to the store."

As the two men turned their backs and walked further down the street, Marlene stood when the cow looked her way. Her first instinct was to go inside and mind her own business. Otherwise, it may lead to trouble she didn't want. Marlene didn't like to draw attention to herself. Ever again. She'd rather hide on this porch forever if it kept her away from the real world. She shuddered at the old memories.

Several townsfolk tried to persuade Clarissa to turn around to no avail. The more Marlene watched, she noticed the animal's irritation when someone took hold of the leather strap around her neck where a loud, annoying bell hung. A clattering noise made her cringe every time the poor thing moved. Why did its owner have to use such a noisy contraption around her neck? It must drive Clarissa crazy. Why did the cow keep her eyes on Marlene? Almost as if the cow was begging her to help. She had that lonely, haunted look in her eye. The one Marlene knew so well. That's when she knew she had to do something.

She looked around to see if anyone came to claim the cow who was now stiffening up, refusing to turn around and go back to its home. Marlene didn't like stepping off her porch, it was a safe haven, but someone had to do something before the cow went temporarily crazy, another place she knew all too well.

Taking in a few short breaths, Marlene forced one foot after another, moving slowly until she was about ten feet away. She stood and looked into the cows eyes, trying to channel the fear she saw there. For some reason the cow was drawn to her. Why? she wondered. She was the most unstable person in Mill Ridge.

The only thing she knew to give herself relief when she became stressed was to focus on her voice. The one thing no one ever was able to take from her. At first, so she didn't scare Clarissa, she began to hum, softly, then a bit louder. The clanging of the bell stopped. She sang out, her voice like a songbirds, taking a step closer so she didn't intimidate Clarissa, who was stressed enough. She hoped and prayed the song would calm her. Marlene knew what is was like to be standing all alone amongst a town full of people and no one was able to help.

Clarissa moved towards her voice. With each syllable, Marlene took a tiny step as the cow slowly came forward. Some folks who were making their way down the street stopped to listen and watch. Marlene knew she had an audience. The hair on her arms stood straight up. Yet, she had to stay focused and not let anything get to her. The cow was more important than people. She had to keep that in her head and concentrate on the animal. She couldn't bear to see the lost, pained look in the cow's eyes any longer. If Marlene had the power to change the animal's circumstances, she would do whatever it took, even if she had to be in the midst of others to do so.

It was a life-changing moment as she reached out to unbuckle the leather strap from the cow's neck. As long as she kept her voice calm and steady, the slow ballad kept Clarissa calm. She petted her head first, rubbing her hands behind the cow's ears. After a few strokes, she reached towards the buckle again, unhitching it. The heaviness astounded Marlene.

The moment the buckle opened, it slid from her neck and began to topple to the ground. Marlene was worried as she reached out to catch it the movement would cause Clarissa to panic. Before the leather hit the ground, a large hand caught it before it fell.

Marlene looked up to see a tall man crouching down, the leather belt in his hand. Strong, muscular arms bulged from the end of a rolled up cotton shirt. She gazed at the man in surprise and caught hazel eyes staring at her. It gave her a jolt. Her throat went dry. He was too close.

When he spoke, his voice was gravely yet kind. "No one has ever gotten so close to her before."

Marlene found her voice. Although she hadn't spoken to anyone in five long years except for her daughter and her brother, she found herself answering him. "Are you the owner?"

He nodded, his eyes still on her. Sweat trickled down her brow but she was frozen, lost in his eyes, unable to lift her fingers to swipe it away. He leaned closer, lifting one hand to wipe the sweat before it fell in her eye. She jerked back, almost stumbling away, a gasp stuck in the deep part of her throat.

Why in the world did she think she'd be able to ever have a conversation with anyone? Especially a man! Swallowing the gut-wrenching scream that tried to come to the surface, she turned and focused on Clarissa, reminding herself to take it one breath at a time. The cow would have to be her saving grace.

Marlene began to hum, softly again, turning away from Clarissa and taking a few steps down the street. There were a few gasps from the onlookers as the cow followed. She felt the animal behind her, even without the loud bell to announce where she was. Whoever placed the bell there hadn't wanted her to get lost. In the end, it had caused more pain for the poor thing than anyone realized.

The owner followed from a few yards away. "She didn't like the bell, did she?"

Marlene shook her head, singing louder, hoping the man would not ask her anything that required more than a shake or a nod.

"She likes you. First time she's taken an interest in anyone. You saved her. She wouldn't let me near her except to milk her twice a day. When I tried to take that blasted bell off, she'd back away so fast I didn't want to get her upset."

She stopped singing for a moment, not understanding his reasoning at all. Anger drew her to speak at last. "Sir, for someone not wanting to upset a cow, you left that bell on to torture her day after day. Clearly, she is much happier without it around her neck." She sped up, singing louder, hopefully to drown out his voice.

The man sighed. He walked faster to catch up. It didn't make sense. One time being uncomfortable while he removed the heavy strap was much better than day after day of endless torture with that bell around her neck, swinging back and forth, causing her to leave her own yard to get away from the noise.

She knew too well how hard it was to get away from the nightmares that haunted her mind.

"She was treated badly. I was afraid to traumatize her."

Marlene stopped. Clarissa stopped on cue. "How so?"

"It was the first day I rode from Wichita Falls to my new home here. Along the trail, a farmer was trying to force her to follow the other three cows. He beat her relentlessly with a whip. I stopped and asked him how long she had the bell around her neck. He had just placed it there. The other three cows didn't mind so much but she was terrified."

A plethora of memories came back to haunt Marlene.

"What did you do?"

"It pained me to see her being mistreated and figured it wouldn't get any better. She was not going to do well. I didn't expect her to stay alive with that strap going to her backside like it was. I offered to buy her. Told the farmer she'd never measure up." He pointed to a rather large two-story white clap-board house at the end of the street. It sat on a corner lot with a white-washed waist-high fence. The gate was wide open, probably the place Clarissa escaped from. "There's my place."

Marlene choked back the sobs that caught at her throat, reliving memories that had been stashed away for the last few years.

She wanted to go back inside her house, the place her brother bought for her and Charlotte to live out their lives. Away from staring eyes. Her safe haven.

He was a hero in her eyes for saving the cow. Yet, it was the trigger that was sending her mind back to where she never wanted to go again. "I have to go," she mumbled, hurrying through the gate so Clarissa followed her. When the cow was inside the yard, she dashed out, waved and ran up the street, away from those hazel eyes, his soft voice and those muscular arms that she wanted to hate but wasn't able to. He hadn't done anything wrong.

He seemed like a normal, upstanding man. Rescuing a cow because its owner was cruel and heartless. Looking at her, not with pity but with a strange curiosity she wasn't able to define. Yet, looks can be deceiving. She knew that better than anyone.

Marlene ignored the other townsfolk as they shouted out to her. The lady they called Elva held the yellow curtain to her bosom while Marlene walked by. She wanted to get inside before anyone else came along. She lifted her skirts and hurried up the street, moving one leg after the other, panting in small spurts as she tried to walk but wanted to run. She looked around to see strange faces smiling at her, some she recognized in passing. She lowered her head, taking care to watch her step as she got closer to home.

Her brother was coming around the corner from the school where he had gone to see Miss Jennie, the schoolmarm. When he noticed how she was trying frantically to get home, he frowned and came towards her, his arms opening wide to protect his sister. He knew she didn't leave the porch much. Mack was the only one who knew what had happened to her.

"That crazy one there!" She heard someone shout out. "The darn cow followed her like nobody's business!"

"She's not crazy! Shut your mouth if you know what's good for you!" Her brother's deep voice warned.

The man in question nodded and called out. "Sorry, Mack! Didn't see you there!"

"Don't tell me, tell her, but not right now." Mack put his protective arms around her, shielding her from any more remarks and helped her inside. He held her for a few minutes, until her heart rate went down.

When she took in a deep breath, he released her. "You okay now, kid?"

She smiled. "I'm not a kid. I'm two years younger than you and you're no kid, either."

He pulled her in for another big brotherly hug. "I'm so glad to hear you talking, Marlene. It about killed me when you stopped."

"I don't talk to anyone else except you and Charlotte. The two of you are the only ones deserving of any conversation." She thought for a moment. "And maybe that man who owns the cow."

Her brother frowned. "Fergenson? What were you talking to him for?"

She twisted her fingers together. "I don't know. He saved Clarissa from a horrible life. Besides, I didn't say more than a few words to him."

Her brother tilted his head and watched her. She didn't like to be scrutinized, especially by Mack. He was a retired Pinkerton agent and was able to read people like nobody's business. She had learned not to show much emotion if she didn't want him to learn anything, even though he usually always figured things out. She wasn't able to hide much from her protective brother.

"Is that a fact?" Mack asked, watching her carefully.

She turned away. "Stop now, Mack. It was an innocent encounter. Clarissa didn't like that bell around her neck."

"I heard you singing. Miss Jennie and I heard it from the stoop at the school house. Charlotte heard it first."

She shrugged like it was no big deal. "I was trying to help Clarissa. No matter what, music is universal. She understood."

"I'm glad you were able to go help someone that needed you. It's a first step, Marlene. You're going to get better. Sooner or later, you'll begin to let people in. Time is all you need."

Marlene shivered. "I don't know, Mack. It's been five years since, well, it's been a long time. I guess I didn't handle things too well."

He frowned again. "You are holding something inside, sis. Something you won't even tell me. Sooner or later, it'll eat you alive if you don't let it out."

Marlene turned away. He was right. No matter what, she'd never tell. Then it wouldn't be real. The horror of that day was a secret she had kept for so long, no one was ever going to get it out of her. No one. It had almost sent her over the edge. To the point where loud noise made her crazy. She had remembered how Mack came to her rescue, trying to put her on a train to Chicago, to take her and Charlotte home with him.

As if she were reliving the moment, she pictured the train and how the people around her sounded so loud, as if they were sitting there, staring at her, screaming at the tops of their lungs. When in fact they were talking amongst themselves. It had been too much too soon and Marlene realized it hadn't been the people around her screaming. It had been her screaming at the top of her lungs. Mack had taken her off the train right away before they hauled her away to the insane asylum.

She owed him so much. He was her sanity when she thought she had lost her mind. He found a nice place for her and Charlotte to stay. The couple took good care of them but she was glad when Mack came and brought them here. This town was different than the big city. It was smaller and the people were not as noisy.

She began to shake.

"Take in deep breaths, Marlene." Her brother knew when she was reliving her past. He was a godsend. She listened to his voice as he breathed with her. She settled down then as exhaustion came over her.

"I need to rest."

Mack helped her to the settee, where he covered her with a blanket. "I'll pick up Charlotte from school, don't you worry. You rest."

Marlene nodded. She was tired. Mack wanted to pick up her baby girl because his love, Jennie, was the school teacher. She was certain Mack wanted to see her again. Besides, she was so tired from all the emotions that played through her head.

She kept seeing Mr. Furgenson's muscular arm as it caught the leather strap and bell before it tumbled to the ground. She saw hazel eyes, curious and engaging as she drifted off to sleep.

<><>

Jack swatted the cow on the behind, talking to her like she was a ten year old child. "Now, Clarissa, you're going to have to behave. There will be no more opening that gate and running off, you hear me?"

"I am sure she does."

Fergenson turned to see the sheriff at the gate. "Well, she needs to be told something. What can I do for you, Sheriff Nightingale?"

He tipped his hat, slid the bolt on the gate open and came through. "Folks keep asking me what it is you do for a living, son. I don't see you going to work each day like the rest of the folks here. I can hardly believe that milk cow gives off enough milk to earn a living from, even though I see you taking the extra to the mercantile each day."

Jack shook his head. Here we go again. "Ain't nobody's business what I do for a living. How do you or anyone else know how much milk this old girl produces? Maybe it's enough for me to live off of."

The sheriff chuckled. "Hardly. I understand you bought the place from the family by proxy when the old man who owned this place died. It's a pretty big space for one person. People have a right to know when someone is being secretive. Especially when you don't come out of that house except to chase Clarissa or bring milk to the store. In Mill Ridge we all have secrets, son. Except we have to know if those secrets will bring trouble."

"No trouble here, sheriff. I can promise you."

The sheriff eyed him carefully. "I'm going to take your word for now. My gut says you're an upstanding citizen. If I'm proved wrong there's going to be a whirlwind of s-"

"There won't be, I promise you that. My word is honorable."

The sheriff tipped his hat and went back through the white-washed gate. A trickle of sweat shot down the side of Jack's neck. He didn't want anyone finding out what he did for a living. If they knew, he'd either be the laughing stock or everyone would be at his door, never leaving him alone.

Nope, it was best no one ever found out.

Chapter 2

Jack walked by Marlene's house several times but she wasn't sitting on the front porch. He hadn't seen the site of her in days. It was almost as if she vanished from the face of the earth. He had to pass by on the way to the mercantile. For the past three days, he had milked Clarissa more than her usual twice a day milking. For some reason, he got an extra one from her.

Clarissa didn't seem to mind though. She chewed on her curd, swatting at flies and enjoying her enclosed space in the back of Jack's yard, which now had a lean-to in the corner to protect her from the elements. She was like a different cow since she got that dang bell off. It was a godsend for Jack, too. He had listened to that blasted bell ringing and clattering all over his yard since he rescued her. Now, it was eerily silent. At least he was able to get his daily work done without the noise.

Walking by Marlene's place one last time, he wondered why she seemed so scared. Her eyes were hauntingly beautiful. But there was history there, as if something terrible had happened. He slowed down as he walked by, wondering when she was going to come back out on the porch.

He had noticed her before. When Mack brought her and the little girl to that house, he had been walking by on his way to the mercantile. She was beautiful in his eyes. Everyone said she had crazy written all over her. Jack didn't believe she was crazy. No. Not with a voice like she had. It was mesmerizing. If it made a cow follow her then there was something beautiful about her. Something special. He wanted to get to know her more. If it were possible.

Disappointment flowed through him when he didn't see her again on his way home. He wondered if she had been a figment of his imagination. Jack shook himself and took longer strides. He needed to get back to work, it was waiting for him.

When he was on the last leg of his walk, a voice so recognizably beautiful made him stop in his tracks. Then he saw her standing at the fence, running her hand along the back of Clarissa's neck while singing to her in that regal voice.

He was unable to move. Even Clarissa stayed still while she sang, except for an occasional swat of the tail. Marlene wore a long cloak with a hood to hide herself. Yet, he knew it was her without seeing her face. There was no way to hide a voice that opened up the heavens like hers did.

When the song was over, she gave Clarissa one last pat. "I must go, sunshine. I'll be back tomorrow." Before she turned, Jack stepped back from the street. She had come here after seeing him go by her house, which made him realize she thought it was safe to come here without him being around. Instead of confronting her, Jack slipped down an alley that ran in between two houses, taking the long way around the block. He wanted her to come back, to sing to his cow and he wanted her to feel safe and wasn't sure why. If Clarissa made her feel safe, he'd stay out of the way. He didn't want to scare her away.

Frustration loomed the rest of the afternoon. Jack tried to sit at his desk and get some work done but every time he tried to put pen to paper, his thoughts fogged up with the image of Marlene, standing outside his home, her beautiful voice serenading his cow. His work had to go out in Friday's post. If it didn't, he didn't get paid. A simple condition of his work he never had trouble meeting before now. The others had warned him about this happening, yet he had always laughed at his associates since it had never happened to him before.

He was wrong for laughing at them. Jack stood, stretched and gazed out the window, trying to get some fresh ideas. Mill Ridge was not as busy as Wichita Falls, where he came in on the train a few months back. He had wanted a more remote place, far away from the big city he had grown up in. This was perfect, even if the town was starting to grow.

He knew Miss Addie was sending mail order brides left and right, causing a plethora of families to sprout up all around. Down the road a few years from now, this town was more than likely to have the rail road tracks passing right by. There'd be more people here, just what he didn't want.

For now, this was the perfect place. It was relatively quiet, especially now that he had that bell off Clarissa's neck, thanks to Marlene. He thought he'd have no trouble working.

Marlene took the place of the distracting bell. All he seemed to be able to do was think of her. He had to get it out of his system, one way or another and get back to work. Walking by her house on purpose or waiting for her to appear was silly. Tomorrow when she showed up to visit with Clarissa, he'd hurry back and speak to her, crossing his fingers she didn't run off.

<> <>

Marlene made a delicious roast with potatoes and an apple pie for dessert. She had spent the latter part of the day cooking after she had been to see Clarissa in the morning. It made her spirit rise up when she sang for the animal. To watch its ears perk up meant the world to Marlene. She was giving back and it made her feel elated. Yet, she knew sooner or later the folks here would make fun of her, whispering behind their bonnets and hands how crazy she was. There were a few who already had said those words.

She had heard it in Dallas, too, how the crazy lady with the child got riled up and screamed at the top of her lungs. From the one incident on the train, she was unable to live down that horrible day. After that, she didn't go outside unless she was hidden from the world under her cloak and hood. Even on the days when it was too hot to wear the coat, she didn't care. If she wasn't able to see others, then she figured they weren't able to see her. Maybe that idea rendered her crazy after all.

At least they had the common courtesy not to make fun or say any slandering remarks when Charlotte was along. With her little blonde curls and delightful smile, everyone fell in love quickly. Charlotte had saved Marlene's life.

Just as she had saved her daughters. Marlene almost stumbled at the thought. She placed a bowl of potatoes on the dining room table, wiping her hands before sitting down. Charlotte looked up at her with a sweet smile. "I'm so hungry my tummy is screaming inside," she told her mother.

Marlene sat across from her at the wooden table. She pressed her hands together in prayer. Charlotte followed suit. "May I say prayers?" she asked, her little eyes dancing with delight.

Marlene nodded.

"Dear God and Jesus, thank you for the food I'm going to eat. My tummy thanks you, too. Oh, and thank you for the big piece of meat and all the other stuff inside the pan. Some of it doesn't look good but I'll try to clean it off my plate. And if I don't, can you tell mommie so she doesn't worry about me eating my vegetables. I love you, God. And all God's children say," she finished, looking at her mother for help.

They both said in unison, "Amen!"

They placed their napkins on their laps and dug in. It was the two of them tonight since Mack was taking Miss Jennie for dinner at the café and a long walk afterwards. Marlene wondered how long it would be until the two tied the knot. Would she still be welcome here? Her brother had promised her she'd always have this home to live in. He meant well, but he had fallen in love now. Things can change so rapidly.

Marlene leaned over to give her daughter a hug. "I'm so glad you are in my life, Charlotte."

"Will you read me a story tonight, Ma? The one about the little girl who was lost in the woods?"

"Of course, dear. After you wash up, we'll get you ready for bed. Would you like to help me with some of the dishes tonight?"

She began to jump up and down, clapping her hands. Marlene tried to give her a stern look but burst out laughing instead. Then she began to bounce up and down until they were laughing so hard Marlene almost fell off the chair.

After her bath and story, Charlotte fell right to sleep. Marlene was restless, so she stewed herself a cup of tea and sat on the porch. It was nice sitting on the rocker, half-hidden behind a large plant she had arranged on a table and a few pots with leafy plants she placed outside. Her brother had nailed a piece of wood from one end of the porch to the other so she was able to set her pots there. She loved flowers. The smell made her calm and looking at them grow made her happy. It also formed a type of wall to the outside world.

She was able to sit out on the porch squeezed between her plants on a wooden bench, without being noticed too much. She knew some of the townsfolk saw her there. They had waved a time or two but mostly everyone let her alone. As long as she didn't talk, they would pass her by with a nod or wave. It was what she preferred.

A lone figure walked down the street towards her porch. It was Mr. Fergenson. Before she realized, she called out. "Hello."

He slowed his pace and gave her a smile. "Why, hello. Is that you, Miss Singleton?"

"It's Miss Everett-Singleton, but you can call me Marlene."

"I will, Marlene. I can't see you but I can hear you. It's almost dark, where are you hiding?" He stood at the front porch trying to peer in. Where he stood all he was able to see was the rows of plants on the thick board Mack had put up. It was almost fun to watch him struggling, trying to find her.

"I'm here."

"Why don't you come out? Then we can talk."

Did she want to talk to him? Obviously, since she was the one speaking out in the first place. Marlene wasn't even sure why she did that. It came out of her mouth like a fly buzzes past your ear. She had to make boundaries first before they talked. "I like my privacy."

He leaned an elbow on the railing. "I can see you do. Interesting. Well, then, we can speak like this. I don't mind."

She was surprised he didn't push the issue. "You don't mind?"

"Not at all. I understand wanting to be alone."

"I've noticed that, Mr. Fergenson. You have a big house all by yourself. It seems odd to live in such a huge house."

"Maybe I intend to have a family someday."

Marlene leaned forward, giving away her hiding spot. "Interesting. How are you going to raise a family if you can't even keep a cow in the yard?"

"Well," he told her, grinning. "That's where you come in."

She stood, shocked at his words. "Me? What in the world do I have to do with anything?"

Was he serious?

"I plan to marry you, Marlene. You just don't know it yet."

"Mr. Fergenson, you are out of line."

He tipped his hat. "Then I best be on my way. My apologies and yet, I'm not sorry I told you. Would you like to take a walk tomorrow after supper?"

Fear cloaked over her like a dark cloud. "I can't possibly go for a walk with you."

He nodded. "Very well, then. Good day, Marlene."

"Good day."

He took a few steps and turned. "You can expect me to ask you every single day until you say yes. I won't stop asking."

When he turned and walked away, she heard the soft sound of his leather shoes shuffling on the ground.

Marlene felt a flush begin to rise up on her cheeks. She placed both hands over her face and closed her eyes. It had been five long years since a man took a real interest in her. She had avoided people all this time. Her husband, Mark, her sweet, darling husband who died so young, was all she'd ever known. She thought life was wonderful when he asked her to marry him, providing them with a rustic, sturdy cabin on a few acres outside of Dallas. They were going to homestead, build a life together but then he left one afternoon and never returned. Her brother, a Pinkerton agent, came to tell her that her husband had drowned in the Brazos River.

She had remembered crying for two weeks straight, not knowing what to do next. Marlene was with child and she was going to tell Mark but never got the chance. For four months, she stayed by herself in that cabin. Her brother was always out on a job. His work took him away for long periods at a time and yet, in between jobs, he always stopped to check in on her. He warned her she should go to the city but she hadn't wanted to leave the home Mark had built for her.

She had gone into town one day for supplies. After buying a newspaper, decided to become a mail order bride. It made sense. It was time to take action. She had kept quiet about the baby, figuring she'd tell her husband-to-be when they met. She had been so naive.

"Marlene, what are you doing out here so late?"

Her brother came up on the porch, a smile as wide as the street itself across his face.

"I'm thinking."

Mack sat down on the small bench beside her. He was tall so he had to push a few of the leaves of the plants scattered here and there out of his way. "Want some company?"

"I always have time for you, Mack." He had been by her side and saved her from a fate worse than death. He still didn't know her darkest secret. It had haunted her dreams for all these years.

"I asked Jennie to marry me." He always got straight to the point.

Marlene gave him a hug. "I bet she said yes."

He smiled and nodded. It was hard for him not to. "She said yes."

"I'm so happy for you, Mack. You deserve to be happy."

He set her back and stared into her eyes with brotherly concern. "So do you. I want you to know you and Charlotte are part of my family. You will live here always. Jennie already told me how she wants you to. She loves Charlotte, so I don't see any issues with all of us in the same house. It's spacious enough."

Marlene let a tear fall. "I knew you were going to ask her, Mack. To be honest, I did worry somewhat."

He returned her hug. "No need to worry. You already like Jennie. She is so busy with her school, I doubt she'll have much time to cook and do all the domestic work that needs done here. I'd appreciate if you'd give her a hand."

Marlene pinched his cheeks in a sisterly manner. "Mack, I know you too well. You don't need me to help out. It's your way of wanting to make sure I'm taken care of. After all, I did go a bit crazy for awhile."

He shook his head. "Marlene, any woman who has been through what you have deserves to be taken care of. I wish I had been there that day," he stumbled with his words.

Mack always got upset when he spoke about the day he found her, clothes torn and filthy from living in the woods for three weeks with a newborn child. She had lived on her instincts, keeping the child warm, shredding her skirts to wrap the child, eating berries and nuts she found. Even stealing supplies from a cabin that happened to be abandoned. She had spent a few nights there, curled up in the corner of the dusty place.

After getting some much needed sleep, Marlene had gone out scouring the area for food. She had worked her way around the near wooded areas, circling the cabin and when she came back around noticed a buck board had pulled up to the front door. The owner had come back.

Marlene left then, going deeper into the wooded area, building a small lean-to from twigs and leaves. It had worked for about five days until the rain began. Texas winds howled at night. Marlene was afraid the baby was getting sick. She had to go back to the real world. Scared and alone, she began to stumble around the woods, trying to find her way out. For a whole day she had wandered until she looked up and Mack was there, his horse galloping towards her and little Charlotte.

She hadn't remembered much after that, waking up a few days later, her child at her bosom. She was in the hospital in Dallas, Mack at her side, who looked as if he hadn't slept in days. She had told him everything, except for the secret she'd take to the grave.

Shaking her head, she realized Mack was waiting for her to comment. "You were there when I needed you, brother. I'll never, ever forget it. But, it's time you moved on from taking care of us and marry that lovely schoolmarm. You two are perfect for each other."

He smiled. "Yes, we are. Thanks, sis. Like I said, this is your home and always will be."

She smiled. "Perhaps I may marry too, again. Someday."

He looked at her in awe. "What did you say?"

"Mr. Fergenson, he told me he was going to marry me."

"Do I need to speak with him?" Mack's voice held a tint of anger.

"No, Mack. Settle down. He mentioned it in passing as he walked by my porch. He wants me to take a walk with him tomorrow."

"That's it. I'm going to warn him now." Mack stood.

She followed suit and placed a hand on his arm. "Please, Mack. Don't be foolish. I like to be asked. Not that I'll go but it was nice to have a good person like him ask."

"I suppose it is. If he gets out of line, you tell me, Marlene and I'll put a stop to any advances."

She gave him a hug before going inside. "Don't worry. I can take care of Mr. Fergenson."

Mack grinned. "I suppose you can."

Chapter 3

Marlene stood at the gate, a hood over her hair like she wore the day before. Jack walked up to her this time instead of hiding in the alley. "Marlene," he said softly so as not to scare her.

She looked startled for a moment that someone would know who she was in her disguise. There was a hitch in her voice then she realized it was Jack and turned back to Clarissa. The cow mooed again, as if Jack was interfering. It almost made him burst out in laughter.

When the song was over, she stood petting Clarissa. He was satisfied to stand beside her, saying nothing at all. When she finally did speak, he was surprised at her words.

"I'll go with you on one condition."

"Anything."

"Anything? You don't know what that condition is." She grinned.

"Does it matter? As long as I have you by my side, I can't go wrong."

"You are a charmer, Mr. Fergenson."

"Jack."

"Jack, it is, then."

"What is your condition?"

"My daughter, Charlotte. She likes to walk. I thought perhaps we can walk her to the church social this evening. We'll be out in the open."

"The church social sounds fine. I'm not too fond of socializing but for you, I'll try anything."

"I'm not either, Jack. I don't care to be around people for long."

He nodded. "I understand. If you tell me you are ready to go, we'll leave immediately."

She pulled her hood closer before turning and walking quickly up the street. Some people turned to stare at her, a confused look on their faces. It was too warm outside for a coat like she was wearing.

Jack wondered how long it would take to convince her she was worth shedding that hooded cloak and walking down the street with her head held high.

He turned around, determined to do the right thing. Jack followed Marlene until she ran up on her porch and quickly went inside. He passed her house and headed towards the school, knowing her brother was there dropping off Charlotte. He had seen him every morning do so. He stood outside the school until Mack came out with a huge smile on his face. When he saw Jack, he sobered.

Mack came towards him. "Fergenson?"

"I come to ask you permission to take Marlene to the church social this evening."

He stared at Jack for more than a minute or so. "I suppose that's up to Marlene."

"She's the one who wants to go. She asked me."

Mack looked surprised. "That a fact? Well, maybe you are good for her. Know this, Jack. I'm watching you. Every move you make that concerns my sister, I'll be right there if you mess up. She's been through too much. Walk softly."

Jack respected Mack. He held out his hand. "I appreciate you looking out for your sister. I plan to marry her, Mack. If she'll have me."

Mack gave it some thought and shook his hand. "You have your work cut out for you. Remember what I said."

Jack sighed when Mack gave him a slap on the shoulder and walked over to the sheriff's office. Word was Mack Everett was going to be the new deputy in town. He had heard the rumors the other day. Guess they weren't rumors after all. Mack walked in the door like he owned the place.

Jack looked at his watch, realizing he had a deadline to meet. He had a day and a half to finish his work and get it out in Friday's mail. Rubbing his palm on his chin, he hurried back to his house. The large two story home loomed over him as he made his way up the path to the front door. He hesitated before going inside. It sure did look like it needed something. What it needed was Marlene and Charlotte and perhaps a few more children.

He grinned. No one back in the city would believe he was ready to settle down. He'd been a loner most of his life, moving from city to city or wherever his job took him. Now, he had finally bought a place where he was able to work at his own pace, away from the hustle and bustle and bright lights.

<> <>

"Do you think I look pretty, mommie?" Charlotte stood in her pink dress and black patent leather shoes. It was one of the special dresses her uncle Mack bought for her when they first moved here.

Marlene twirled her around in a circle. "You look beautiful, young lady. Like a princess." Charlotte's eyes widened and she giggled.

"Mommie, that's silly. Princesses have crowns."

"I can make one for you," Marlene offered, knowing Charlotte's next move would be to wrinkle her nose. And she did.

"My two favorite ladies look lovely this evening," Mack told them. Jennie was standing alongside of Mack, her arm through his.

"I swear if I hadn't met you already, Miss Charlotte, I'd swear you were the princess of Mill Ridge."

Charlotte giggled again, her cheeks pinkening at the compliment from Miss Jennie. She curtseyed and ran to the door when someone knocked. It had to be Jack. Knowing it was him, no one reprimanded her for opening the door.

"Well good evening, Miss Charlotte. You look like a princess," Jack told her out of the blue. Marlene smiled when she heard Charlotte giggling.

"We're all waiting for you! Hurry in so we can go." Charlotte took him by the hand and pulled him in to the others. "He's here! Can we go now?"

Marlene and Jack each held one of Charlotte's hands as they all made their way to the church social. She was awfully happy this evening. "I get to have a pretend daddy, don't I, mommie? Now the kids won't ask me where my daddy is."

She was about to explain that Jack wasn't her daddy when he placed a finger over his lip above the little girl's head.

She frowned, not wanting to give her daughter any false hopes. They'd been fine the last five years, the two of them. But when Jack looked into her eyes, she felt the fear slide away. Was she able to trust this man? She hardly knew him.

She took a hand to pull her cloak closer when she realized she had left the house without it. How did she manage now? There was no place to hide. As they walked on to the grass at the church, most of the townsfolk were there. Some mingled in small groups while others sat on benches holding a plate of food. Soft music played in the back ground. She looked up to see a man playing a fiddle, singing softly. It was very nice.

She felt exposed. Charlotte let go of her hand to run off with the other kids who were playing games in front of the church steps. Before she realized what happened next, Jack's soft hand encased hers in his own. She almost jumped two feet in the air.

Instead of letting go, he held on. "I didn't mean to frighten you." His words came out softly, against her ear as he spoke for her only.

Marlene sighed. She needed to get over this fear. It had its hand around her neck like a vice. "I get anxious in crowds. I'm not sure I'm ready for this."

He gazed into her eyes. Somehow, she didn't feel alone. It was as if he knew her fear. She took in a few deep breaths.

"Fear is not going to hurt you. Not ever again. I am here to keep fear away. I don't know what happened, Marlene, all I know is I don't want you to ever have to face things alone. Will you let me help you?"

His words floored her. She wanted to sink to the ground and cover her face with her hands but his words made her pull her shoulders back and her chin up. "I can do this. Jack, lead the way."

He tucked her arm in his and they moved forward. She realized with someone by her side, it wasn't as bad as she had imagined. There were even some folks who seemed pleasantly surprised she made it to the social.

"We're glad you are here," Sophie Nightingale told her. She gave her a hug and moved on to the next person. The sheriff's wife was mingling among all the guests.

Doc Hart and his wife Caroline shook hands with Jack, then turned to Marlene. "How are you feeling, Marlene?" Doc Hart asked.

What he meant was she able to handle being around all these people. When she first got here, Mack insisted she have a physical exam done. Then Doc Hart spent over an hour talking with her since Mack told him what had happened. He was understanding and kind. He told her how his wife had a serious problem with migraines and everyone in her home town thought she was a witch because it caused her to have epileptic seizures. He had wanted her to know she wasn't alone, that everyone had problems. He didn't make her feel like an outcast for being scared around people. "I'm doing fine so far, Doc."

Her words sounded weak. She took a deep breath. This was challenging for sure. Then she realized Jack had a hold of her hand when he squeezed it lightly. He seemed to know when she needed his encouragement.

Doc Hart seemed pleasantly surprised when she talked. He hadn't heard her speak before. "Good for you, Marlene." He acknowledged Jack and moved along. Caroline squeezed her hand and gave her a wink.

"Would you like some dessert?" Jack asked, moving to a bench under one of the large trees. It was in sight of everyone and yet away from the center of the crowd, another kind gesture to keep her from getting too anxious.

"That would be lovely, thank you." He understood her need to go slowly. As he walked towards the tables filled with food, Marlene watched in amusement as Mack slapped him on the back and said something to him. He was probably warning Jack to behave. When Jack just nodded, she knew everything was going to be OK.

Charlotte played with the other kids until Marlene caught her eye and motioned for her. The little girl dragged her feet, knowing it was time to go. She kept looking back at the kids, waving whole-heartily.

Jack was sitting on the bench beside her, quiet. He had given her space to get accustomed to everything. She looked at him. "Thank you. It's been a lovely evening."

He stared at her, those hazel eyes penetrating so she wasn't able to look away. "I'd like to see you again, Marlene."

She shivered and wanted to tell him she wasn't what he thought. Marlene had evil inside of her that no one was aware of. She had done a horrible thing. Not even her brother knew. No one did. If Jack got too close, he may find out about her nightmares that caused her to curl up in her bed, shivering not from the cold but from what she did.

Was Marlene willing to take the risk?

When Charlotte arrived, Jack picked her up and set her on his shoulders. She was so excited she yelled out to all her friends. "Look at me!" Her hands were moving back and forth, she was laughing and it made Marlene's heart melt.

He held out his hand for Marlene. "Let me walk you home." As they left the social, she was trying to decide if she'd accept his offer to meet again.

When Charlotte laughed so hard tears rolled down her cheeks at something Jack said, Marlene knew it was all worth it to hear her squeal with delight. It was worth every single, dark secret to see her baby girl happy. For now, she'd see what happens and keep those horrible memories tucked deep, deep away where no one was allowed to go.

<> <>

"Did you hear what I said!"

Jack had been day dreaming as he stood in front of the postal counter. Jack stared at the skinny man.

"That'll be four dollars."

Jack thought it was an outrageous price to send mail to New York City but he didn't want to draw any attention. If anyone were to open the package by mistake, it would be the end of things for him, so he wasn't about to make a fuss. He wasn't ready yet. Maybe soon, but not yet. He threw some coins on the counter, added an extra for a tip and left without delay. He wanted to stop by and see if Marlene was up for a walk this evening.

When he got closer to her front porch, she was already outside, leaning over the railing and waving him down.

When he got there, he tipped his hat. "Well, it's a fine day now, isn't it, Marlene."

"It sure is. I wanted to tell you I was with Clarissa this morning and her one foot seemed to be hurting. She limped across the yard when I got there."

He didn't like the sound of things. "I'll have to have the doctor take a look at her."

Marlene looked worried. "She hasn't left the yard since we took off the silly bell. There must be something there causing the damage. Maybe we need to check. I can come with you."

"It will be a pleasure."

He held out his arm, feeling lucky to have her with him so soon after the church social the other night. They made their way across the street and stopped to see Doc Hart. He was having dinner with his wife but when he heard the news of Clarissa, he promised to stop by within the hour.

They hurried towards Jack's house. He noticed Marlene wasn't wearing her cloak. Her hair was held back with silver pins along the side while the curls laid loose down her back. Jack almost stumbled when he realized he wasn't paying attention.

Marlene shook her head. "Jack, you are staring at me all the time. Can you please stop?"

"It's hard to. You are so beautiful."

She smiled and hurried ahead of him. "Now is not the time, Jack." Opening the gate, Clarissa began to step across the yard. Jack saw her right front leg had a slight limp.

"I can't believe I didn't take notice this morning." He had been in a hurry to get to the post office and never noticed Clarissa's state of affairs. Jack felt bad he had not paid attention. "I'm sorry, Clarissa." A hand began to rub her behind her ears while Marlene hummed a slow tune. Before long, Doc Hart came along with his medical bag.

After her exam, the doc nodded his head and placed Clarissa's hoof back on the ground. "It looks like she has some foot rot."

Marlene gasped. "What is that?"

"It comes from bacterium Fusiformis necrophorus or an infected foot. Lucky for you, Jack, you got it in the early stages. Good call."

Jack spoke up. "I have to admit I didn't notice. Marlene did."

Doc Hart nodded to her. "We'll clean it out and give her some ointment every day for awhile and see what happens." He looked at the make-shift lean-to. "What kind of hay do you have in there, Jack?"

He shrugged. "I got it from the sheep farmer that came through. He had an abundance when he was hauling it through town."

"My advice is to get rid of all that hay and start over. It's probably where she got the foot rot. Sheep tend to spread the disease more than anything. Never, Jack, ever buy hay from a sheep farmer."

Lesson learned. Marlene stayed and helped Jack hold Clarissa while the doc cleaned the infection from the foot. She sang to the cow, keeping her as calm as possible. Every now and again she felt a swat when Clarissa swiped her tail across the air. She couldn't help but giggle when Clarissa hit Jack in the back of the head.

He grinned, moving his head the next time the tail came his way. Instead, it hit the doc on the head but he didn't seem to mind. It didn't even seem to phase him.

"All done." Doc Hart stood and handed a jar of ointment to Jack. "You need to put this on her foot twice a day, morning and night for about a week. That should heal it up. I'll come back and check on her next Friday."

Even though Doc Hart wasn't an animal doctor, he still looked after them. He didn't have to but he did. Marlene waved as he left.

"Well, let's get to work." She clapped her hands together. "I'll need a pitchfork."

"You want to help me get rid of the hay?"

"I sure do. Come on, Jack. You afraid of a little hard work?"

He rolled up his sleeves. "That sounds like a challenge!" Behind his house, a small shed held several pitchforks and shovels. He handed her one. "Let's throw the hay in a pile over the fence. Since no one owns that land yet, we'll burn the hay so no one else gets sick from it."

Marlene didn't wait for him to tell her any more. She stuck the pitchfork in the hay and flung it over the fence. Over and over, the two worked diligently until there was no more hay in the lean-to.

Jack went inside and brought two glasses of water. He also had a box of matches to burn the hay. It flared up with a whoosh. The two drank their water and watched the pile burn. Even Clarissa moseyed over to stand beside Marlene. She reached out and scratched behind the cow's ears. Poor thing, if they hadn't caught the infection, she may have died.

Jack was mesmerized. He wanted to kiss her. He had no choice. Knowing she feared men for some reason, he was trying hard to be gentle. He needed to kiss her.

He sighed and looked into her beautiful face.

<><>

Jack gazed into her eyes then, those hazel orbs telling her things he wasn't able to say. Was she falling for him? It was impossible. She had so many issues to figure out. The more she tried to shield herself from falling for another man, the more her feelings of hate inside were beginning to fade.

What was happening to her? She had been determined to live out her life a widow, protecting Charlotte from all the bad men she knew existed. The flames rose up, burning the infected hay while Jack kept staring at her as if he wanted to kiss her.

She was mesmerized. Dare she allow another man to kiss her? No one had tried in five years. The last kiss she ever had was the one where, oh dear Lord, no! Don't let me remember that right now! She had to squash those horrible memories. This wasn't the time or place for them to surface.

Her heart began to beat faster. She stepped back from Jack, who took a step closer. He dipped his head and leaned in, covering her mouth with his own. Her mind wanted to scream, to move away, push him, but when he touched her lips she was drawn into him. It wasn't like that kiss with that horrible man.

It wasn't bad at all.

He was gentle.

A soft kiss upon her lips.

She sighed.

She took a small step closer.

Jack wrapped his arms around her shoulders. He was so gentle as if he knew she was scared.

She brought her arms up, around his waist, barely touching him.

He deepened the kiss, pulling her even closer.

Marlene's head was spinning. The kiss was delightful, special and she was glad he didn't let her fear keep him from kissing her. She needed this. Marlene needed to know not all men were animals. There were good men, too.

It had been a shame the last one had tried to have her killed.

Charlotte too.

<h1 style="text-align:center">Chapter 4</h1>

For the next week, Marlene was so busy she barely had time to breathe. First thing after getting Charlotte off to school, she'd hurry to help Jack tend to Clarissa's foot. It had become their routine after a few days. She'd hum and sing to the animal as Jack tended to her foot. She looked forward to seeing him each day. In the evening, after supper, Jack stopped by to escort her and Charlotte to see Clarissa. Even the cow was starting to wait by the fence for their visit.

Charlotte wanted to ride the cow. Jack and Marlene laughed so hard the one evening when she tried to climb on. After a scolding, the little girl didn't try it again. She even gave Clarissa a hug and said she was sorry.

Jack scratched his head. "I tell you what, Charlotte. The old owner of this house had a wooden rocking horse. I believe it's in one of the rooms upstairs. Would you like to come inside and we'll see if we can find it? You can ride that without any problems."

Charlotte jumped up and down clapping her hands. "Yes, can we, Mommie?"

Marlene looked around. The streets were fairly empty this time of the evening. Maybe one or two townsfolk sitting on their porches. "I guess no one will take issue to us going inside, since we have the child along."

They followed Jack inside to a wide open foyer with a large staircase that led to the second floor. It was quite extravagant. On the outside, it looked like a simple, white-washed two story house.

"Wow!" Charlotte said, her voice so loud it echoed through the high ceilings. She laughed so hard when the echo continued.

After a few more times, the three were calling out names and words that echoed back to them.

Jack's laughter was so refreshing. She watched him as he carried on with Charlotte, calling out words with a deep voice and then changing it up to a high pitched one. He would be a great father. Her heart hurt at the thought she was moving on from her husband Mark. She had only been married to him less than a year before he had died. The man had been reckless, going out on the river when the weather was bad. He had been told not to.

His carelessness had left her with a child to raise alone. After realizing she had no skills to make her own way, Marlene had sent a letter to the mail-order agency to become a mail order bride. After several letters, she met with her future husband-to-be in Dallas. Her brother had told her not to do anything foolish, he'd make sure she was taken care of. But she didn't listen, not wanting to depend on him. Besides, he wasn't home much, always on the road doing Pinkerton work. No, she had to make her own decisions.

The day she met up with John Abbott was when the horror began. The insulting kiss he bestowed upon her should've warned her then. She sighed. No sense in recreating something that had been put to rest five years ago. In time, she'd forget. She hoped.

"Mommie, come on." Charlotte held out her hand, bringing Marlene back to focus on the reason she was here. It did no good to think of the past. Not when things were going so good.

Jack took them into another room to the right, a parlor. "I'll be right back." They sat down while he went upstairs. Charlotte kept bobbing up and down on the settee.

"Please, no bouncing, Charlotte."

The little girl tried so hard to stop. "Yes, ma'am." Then she whispered in her mother's ear. "I'm so excited I want to scream!"

Marlene smiled at the girl. "Patience is a virtue, my child. No more bouncing."

While they waited, Marlene gazed around the small, neat parlor. There was a square wooden table alongside the settee, with several books and newspapers. Marlene picked up a small book with some feisty looking characters on the front. She realized it was a dime novel. She remembered seeing some at the news-stand in Dallas but never up close.

When she picked it up, the pages were thin, and the large words of the title made her curious. *The Secret Revengers or Tales of four brothers in pursuit of a killer! by J. Fergy.* Marlene studied the front page carefully. Then she turned the page. *Come along with the four Winston brothers as they seek vengeance for the murder of their father. In the next episode, the boys discover a secret hide-a-way. Then, Bill comes across one of the gang members who shot and killed their father. Will they be able to catch the varmint? Be sure to stay tuned and buy the next instalment.*

When Jack entered the room with the wooden horse in his arms he stopped in his tracks and frowned. Marlene glanced up right then and wondered why he wasn't smiling. She watched as his eyes were on the book she held. Had she been too bold to pick it up without asking? Was she being rude? She placed the book on the side table and stood. Embarrassed, she waited quietly while Charlotte ran over to Jack.

"Is that the horsey?"

Jack quickly looked away, changing his frown to a smile. He knelt down to Charlotte's level and began to show her how to get on the wooden horse. It was just her size. She held onto the wooden handle and rocked back and forth. "Look at me, Mommie! Look Jack! I'm riding a pony!"

For the next half hour while Marlene rode the wooden pony, Jack seemed thoughtful. He didn't say much at all. She tried to make light conversation but he answered her without looking at her the way he usually did. He seemed so distracted. Was it something she had done?

"I think we better get home," she told Charlotte. Of course, the young girl complained that she didn't want to leave.

Jack spoke up. "It will be here for you tomorrow when you arrive to check on Clarissa. You can ride it again, OK? Now, your mother wants to get you home."

"Thank you." Marlene accepted his nod and helped Charlotte as they made their way outside. Jack accompanied them to their front porch and said good night.

"I'll see you both tomorrow," he told them, not looking at Marlene.

She didn't want him to leave on a sour note. "Charlotte, go on inside. I'll be right behind you." When she did as told, Marlene turned to Jack who was ready to walk away. "Have I done something wrong, Jack? You don't seem yourself tonight."

He stuffed his hands deep in his pockets and sighed. "I'm sorry, Marlene, it's not you. It's been a long day and I'm feeling under pressure from my work."

"Oh, Jack! Are we too distracting? We don't have to come visit Clarissa in the evenings if you have work to do." Although, she was hoping he still wanted her there. She enjoyed how he picked her up and they all walked together like a family.

"Not at all, Marlene. You can never be distracting to me. I've got some thinking to do and then we'll talk. Can we go to supper together in a few days, just the two of us?"

"Of course. I'll ask Jennie and Mack to keep Charlotte on Monday evening. Although, it may be hard to tear her away from the wooden horse. I have a feeling she's going to want to come over every single day. Now that Clarissa is pretty well healed, we don't really need to visit daily."

"Yes, you do. It's good for you and for your daughter. And, for me." He took his hand out of his pocket and brushed it across her cheek. "And for Clarissa. She loves you. Goodnight, Marlene."

She watched as he turned and walked back to his place. There was something wrong, she just wasn't sure what.

Jack wanted to kick himself in the foot. When he saw her pick up the dime novel he froze. Would she put two and two together and realize he was the author of that book? He had been writing under the pen name J. Fergy. Then someone found out who he was. After what had happened to his sister, he never, ever wanted anyone to know.

Now, he was afraid she'd find out. If he married her, Marlene would learn the kind of work he did. He didn't see that he could keep it a secret from her even though he wanted to. Was that putting her in danger? He had tried to forget about the past and succeeded until he saw her holding the dime novel in her hands. Then, everything from the past flashed in front of him. His sister. Her death. All because of his work as a writer of published work.

He strolled past his house, past the field where they burned the hay and out of town. He needed to think. The darkness of the night would cloak him like Marlene's coat and hood did her. He wanted Marlene but didn't want her to know what he did for a living. This job had cost him so much. He had been through too much, blamed himself for his sister's death. If he married Marlene, he had to tell her everything. When he had told her he was going to marry her, for a brief time he forgot what had happened. Until he saw Marlene sitting there holding the book. Then it all came back like a Texas tornado destroying everything in its path.

He thought about telling her now, before he proposed. Except, what if she refused his marriage proposal? There would be one more person who knew about him. Could he really take that chance? He knew her to be honest and held secrets of her own, and yet, did he know her well enough to trust her?

Luckily, his editor and publisher, Mr. Beadle, was sworn to secrecy. It was the only way Jack agreed to continue to write the dime novels and newspaper articles required of him. He had that in writing, in the contract they both signed before he left New York City. His location was never to be exposed.

Jack walked for over an hour before turning back around. He knew it was going to be a long night. He walked past Clarissa, who was sitting down near the fence. She made a noise as he went by, causing him to stop and pet her. The cow's presence made him think of Marlene and how the first time he saw her, truly saw her, she was singing her heart out to this cow, to soothe and calm the poor thing. Marlene had a heart of gold. He wanted her for his wife. Yet, he was scared. From the moment he saw her holding the dime novel in her hands, he realized he may not be the right man for her.

It broke him in two.

"What do I do, Clarissa? What the Sam hell do I do?"

<> <>

Every evening Jack continued to pick up Charlotte and Marlene, walking hand in hand to visit with Clarissa. Then, they'd go inside while Charlotte played on the wooden horse and have a glass of lemonade. Marlene noticed the pile of books and newspapers were no longer on the table by the settee. For some reason, the book she had held in her hands had upset Jack. Why? He had looked at her with a sadness she only felt when she thought her daughter was lost. She pushed that thought deep, deep down inside. There was no way she wanted to think of that time in her life or she'd lose her mind for sure.

The doctors in Dallas had wanted her to talk about what had happened to her. What they had wanted to do was send her to an insane asylum but as long as Mack was in charge, he told them no. The couple he hired to take care of them tried to get her to speak and became frustrated when she refused. They had treated both her and Charlotte well enough but she knew they wanted the two of them gone. The day her brother came to bring them both here was a glorious day she'll never forget. It was as if the past was no longer biting at her soul. No, she left the past in Dallas. Coming to Mill Ridge was a new start, one that didn't include the horror of what happened. She had to learn to let it go, for her sake as well as her daughter.

She knew there was something eating at Jack. Something huge. There was something from his past, like hers, he wanted to forget and move on from. She sensed it was a struggle for him. Why did she think it had to do with the book she had held in her hand the other day?

Marlene sighed. He had been slowly bringing her out of her shell, day after day, unwilling to give up on her. She didn't wear her cloak any more, there was no reason to hide. Jack was slowly giving her the confidence back she had lost. Now, he was backing away.

She looked up to catch him watching her. Marlene gave him a smile. "I think we best get home."

He stood, tearing his eyes away like it was a hard thing to do. He collected Charlotte and they walked back to her house.

"Goodnight, girls."

Charlotte tugged on his hand. He leaned down while Marlene watched in awe as she gave him a kiss on the cheek. Her little hand reached up and rubbed in the kiss. "I wish you were my daddy," she said before she turned and skipped through the front door.

Marlene gasped. Jack stood up, speechless while his face grew pale. Marlene knew he had a hard time responding. What she witnessed was so precious and yet she didn't want to get Charlotte's hopes up. Jack may not want to marry her now. Did she even want to marry him? He was so distant that she didn't know if he had changed his mind. It was all too confusing.

"I have to go. Goodnight, Marlene." He turned abruptly, his shoes making the same soft noise, only faster. Marlene leaned over the porch rail to see him picking up speed, then he was hurrying towards his house, past his house and into the darkness. He must be upset at Charlotte's words.

She'd have to talk to her daughter. The child meant well and yet it wasn't in her place to say such things. This was getting complicated all around. Her daughter was falling in love with a man she wanted for her daddy. Marlene was finally starting to feel comfortable in public, wanting to spend more time with Jack. Her brother and Jennie were getting married. Soon, she'd feel like a third wheel in their home, even though no one would ever ask her to leave.

She didn't want to be an old maid. Marlene stood on the porch, contemplating her next move. Perhaps it was time to speak to Jack about the whole situation. Except she wasn't about to go running down the street into the dead of night to find him. In the morning, that's when she'd tell him they needed to talk. This wasn't going to wait until their supper on Monday.

Except on Friday, she had forgotten the doctor was visiting again to check up on Clarissa. Not much after she got to Jack's house, Doc Hart showed up. She sang to Clarissa while he examined her.

He stood up, placing the hoof on the ground. "She looks healed. Everyone did a fine job taking care of her." Doc Hart turned to Jack. "I know you care about this old girl and she is supplying you with your means of income through her milk. Have you ever thought of sending her to one of the local farms where she'd have more space to roam free? This yard is pretty confined, Jack."

Jack nodded. "I don't need the income from her milk, Doc. I've been thinking about it for awhile now. I got used to her being around and didn't want to send her somewhere where she'd be treated badly like the farmer I bought her from."

Doc Hart snapped his bag shut. "I have the perfect place for her. My sister Annabelle and her husband Grant have a a small farm beside the Holloway Ranch. Plenty of space there for Clarissa."

Jack shuffled his feet. "She means a lot to Charlotte. I don't want to sell her."

"Let me talk to my sister. I'm heading up there this afternoon. Perhaps you can keep her there for a small pittance. She really needs wide open fields, Jack."

Marlene watched the myriad of emotions play across his face. He knew the right thing to do was to set Clarissa free where she was able to roam and eat grass and not be confined in a small area. She looked at Jack. "We can arrange a weekly outing to go visit her if that is acceptable to the doctor's sister. What do you think?"

Doc Hart spoke up before Jack had a chance to reply. "I know my sister will not mind. She loves company, too. I'll stop by after my visit and let you know. Good day." He tipped his hat and let himself out of the gate.

"I think that settles things. Jack, you know the right thing to do is to give her the space she needs."

He nodded. "Are you talking about Clarissa?"

Marlene shuffled her feet. "Why, yes. Who else would I be speaking of?"

He grinned. "No one, I guess."

Marlene thought that was an odd statement for him to make as she made her way back to her house. She had a ton of work to do and wanted to do some cooking this afternoon. It helped keep her mind occupied when she stayed busy.

Marlene had learned to make some pretty delicious sweets when they lived in Dallas. The couple they lived with thought it would be good for her to keep her mind occupied and they were right. It was a skill she enjoyed. Perhaps someday she'd open a sweet shop filled with confections and baked goods here in Mill Ridge. Wouldn't that be something, that's if she overcame her fear of people completely.

What Jack had done for her already was a good start, but she had a long way to go. Throwing on her apron, Marlene set out the ingredients she needed for some delicious molasses candy. She got the stove going, heating it to just the right temperature and placed a pot on top. Adding two cups of water and a cup of molasses, she let it boil, day dreaming about Jack as she stirred the concoction. When it thickened, she added a dollop of butter the size of an egg and a teaspoon of vanilla. Well, her idea of a teaspoon. Marlene didn't really measure too well since she made her candy by tasting it as she cooked.

While it was cooking, she place a bowl of cool water on the table, went to the pantry behind the kitchen area and opened the ice box for a few slivers of ice to keep the water cool. That's what stiffened the sweet treat. She wondered if Jack liked candy? A smile crossed her face thinking of him.

Once everything was blended, she took it off the stove and dropped a little in the ice cold water. The creamy thick piece turned brittle, exactly the way she wanted it to do.

"Perfect!" She repeated her efforts over and over again until she had half the table covered in chunks of brittle molasses candy. Charlotte would be in sweet heaven with all this! She'd wait until her daughter came home from school and let her place the sweets in tins, that will give it plenty of time to harden to perfection.

Before she cleaned up her mess, Marlene took a break and poured herself a glass of lemonade, taking to the porch for some outside air. It was late afternoon, the busiest time of the day in Mill Ridge when folks got off work or finished up their purchases at the mercantile. She could see a good portion of Main street from where she sat. No longer wanting to hide behind all of her plants and flowers, Marlene had pulled a chair closer to the front of the porch.

She wasn't surprised any longer when a few of the townsfolk called her by name.

"Good afternoon, Marlene," the sheriff called out from across the street. She waved to him before he went back inside.

Yes, things were changing. She was starting to come out of her shell.

Was she good enough to marry a man like Jack? That is, if he asked? He told her he was going to marry her. Except now, Jack was acting standoffish and she didn't know why. She had wanted to discuss things with him but the opportunity hadn't arrived. Perhaps she'd have to wait until Monday after all.

Chapter 5

Marlene was getting ready to go inside when the man she had been thinking about approached. He was coming back down the street with his empty milk pail and stopped when he saw her.

"Doc Hart said his sister will let Clarissa board on their farm for one dollar a month."

"That's wonderful! I'd take her up on the offer."

"Plus, she'll make sure she gets milked and distribute it to the farm workers. That will free me up from having to milk her several times a day."

Marlene thought it was a shame because she'd miss seeing him when he walked by each day. She'd miss the evenings more, when her and Charlotte went to visit the animal.

"Would you and Charlotte like to help me get her there tomorrow morning? It's about a half hour ride to their farm. Doc gave me directions."

"We would love to accompany you. Charlotte will be thrilled. Hold on, I'll be right back." Marlene ran in the house, rummaging through a cupboard and found a small burlap sack. She placed a handful of the hard candies in the bag, tied it up and went back outside. "Here."

He looked pleased. "What's in the bag?"

"Well, why don't you look."

Jack, smiling, unravelled the tie and peeked inside. "My weakness," he told her, his smile getting bigger. He reached in and popped a rather large piece in his mouth. Closing his eyes, he chewed on the molasses candy for over a minute until Marlene began to giggle.

"I think you are attracting attention." His moans had a few townsfolk turning their heads, looking puzzled at Jack standing there looking like that.

He tied up his bundle. "They can't have any!"

Just as he spoke, Charlotte came ripping around the corner, Mack in tow. "Jack! Jack! Hello, Jack!"

He leaned down and Charlotte jumped in his arms. Marlene was getting concerned. She didn't want Charlotte to get too upset if Jack decided not to marry her. Even though her brother was always in the little girl's life, Charlotte was trying to bond with a man she wasn't sure wanted the same thing. She didn't ever want her little girl to suffer any sadness in her life. Marlene would make sure of it one way or another. When she looked up she saw her brother watching the two with the same wary look. No doubt she'd hear about it from Mack, too. He was overprotective at times.

Jack stood and patted Charlotte on the head.

"What do you have in the bag?" her little voice asked.

"Would you like to see?"

She nodded, her curls bouncing around. At least she was standing still, not jumping up and down like she normally does.

Jack opened the burlap bag. "Go ahead, put your hand in."

Charlotte trusted him completely and dug in without worry. Marlene almost let a tear slip down her cheek at their antics. She pulled out a piece of candy. Her eyes widened and when she popped one in her mouth, she giggled.

"You are silly, Jack. These are my mommies!"

Marlene laughed out loud. Her daughter knew her well. "There's a whole table full inside, little one. I'll bet you'd like to help put them in tins, wouldn't you?"

That's when she began jumping up and down.

"Settle down first. Why don't you go inside and start. I'll be right in. There is a tin on the table for you to fill."

Charlotte waved while bouncing and heading inside, her little feet were speeding through the door before anyone could say another word. It made Marlene's heart warm to see her child so happy. That's all she'd ask for, nothing more. If Jack decided not to ask for her hand, she'd still be happy.

Heartbroken on one hand but happy her daughter was finally settled and in a place she loved. The city was not for them. Dallas was too much, it had brought out the worst of Marlene and she recognized it as such. No. Here is where she wanted to be. Alone, if that's all she'd ever have.

"Good day, then, Marlene, Mack," Jack nodded to each. "I'll be by later for our walk."

She sighed. This evening would be the last time they'd all three walk to see Clarissa. Then what?

Mack watched her closely. She always was aware when he had something on his mind. "Out with it, brother. What have you been observing with your eagle eye?"

"You know me well."

"I sure do." She placed her hands on her hips. "You may as well get it off your chest before you explode."

He agreed. "I am worried about you, Marlene. You and Jack seem to be hitting it off just fine except there is a mystery about him I want you to be cautious about. Several folks in town have wondered themselves."

She shrugged. "Honestly, Mack, what's to worry about? He's a good man. You know the kind of men I've dealt with. He is an angel compared to them."

Mack waved a hand. "That's not what I mean. Just be careful before you make any rash decisions. People wonder how he's making a living besides selling the cow's milk."

"It's not anyone's beeswax, to be honest."

"I worry he's doing something illegal. Every Friday he sends a package through the mail. People say it seems mysterious. I don't want you and Charlotte in the middle."

"You have a license to investigate, sir. Why don't you try to find out." She was being facetious but the look on his face made her realize he was itching to put his skills to use again. "No, Mack, don't you dare!"

He grinned. "You said I should."

She picked up her skirts and turned to go inside. "Mack Everett, you stay out of my business. I'm a grown woman and if I wanted you to snoop around, I'd have asked. I trust Jack."

Mack followed inside, not saying a word. The gears in his mind were already turning, she could tell. It probably didn't hurt to make sure Jack was an up and up citizen. Had anyone ever asked him what he did for a living?

Perhaps someone should.

She knew her brother.

He was one of the Pinkerton's finest agents until he retired.

Once he was on a case, he didn't stop until the truth was revealed.

She had to put a stop to his snooping before that happened.

She'd ask Jack himself. If he were honest, he'd tell her the truth. If there was a truth to tell.

<> <>

Later that evening when Jack came to call, Marlene didn't want to ruin their last day visiting at Jack's place with Clarissa with a ton of questions about his work. First, they had to explain to Charlotte about the decision made for the animal's well being. Perhaps another time she'd ask him about his work. They had time.

After Charlotte was done petting Clarissa, she became restless. "Mommie, can we go inside now and ride the wooden horsey?" Clarissa was bouncing already.

"Well, first, we'd like to talk to you about Clarissa."

"Clarissa?"

"Yes, Clarissa. Jack, would you like to explain?" When their eyes met, she felt a bond so strong it pulled her towards him. Not in a physical way, but as if they understood they wanted the same thing. As if he understood her need to help her daughter understand the cow wasn't going away forever. She blinked her eyes, trying to wish it away.

"Sure. Charlotte, we learned from the doctor that Clarissa needs more space to stay healthy. And, we want her to always be healthy and never sick, right?"

Charlotte nodded. "Oh, yes, Jack. With all her milk she is healthier than anybody in this world!"

He squatted down to her level and laughed. "That's true, she is healthy. We want to keep her like that and by taking her to Doc Hart's sister's farm, she'll be able to have a large area to eat grass and make lots of milk. I'm afraid my back yard isn't big enough for her any more."

At first Charlotte looked devastated. "I won't get to see her after school?" Her lower lip formed a pout.

Jack smiled. "Of course you will. We will be allowed to visit her any time we like. I was thinking we can go every Saturday morning. How does that sound to you?"

Charlotte reached out a hand and put it on his cheek. "Will she have other kids to visit her all the rest of the times?"

"Yes, Annabelle has some children on the farm. I'm sure if you ask them tomorrow when we take her, they will be happy to keep an eye on Clarissa for you."

Charlotte gave Jack a hug. "I can't wait! I want Clarissa to have a big, big, big yard! Now can we go inside to play on the rocking horse?"

They both laughed. "Of course." Jack stood and took her hand, then held out his other hand for Marlene. She took it as they went inside. They were like a family. Was Marlene prepared to risk it all for Jack to be a part of their lives? Her and Charlotte were a packaged deal. She had fought too hard to make sure of it.

She was so tired of the past and how it had a hold on her. Sometimes she just wanted to blurt it all out, what had happened that night except she was scared to death. Yet, Jack made her feel things she had never felt before. He was slowly bringing her around.

As she sat in the parlor while Charlotte played on her wooden horse, Marlene smiled at Jack when he brought her a glass of lemonade. He sat down beside her, not asking for permission.

Usually, Jack sat across the room in a wing back chair with plenty of room between them. Now, he was so close, she wasn't sure she'd be able to breathe properly.

"Marlene, we have to talk."

"I was thinking the same thing."

He frowned. "You were?"

She nodded. "Yes, I don't think it is appropriate this evening but perhaps Monday when we go to supper."

He agreed. "That sounds fair. Although, I wonder what is on your mind at this moment??

Did he scoot over a tad closer? Marlene swore she hadn't smelled the scent of his cologne before. Now, it was clinging to her nostrils. She took in a deep breath.

He turned to her as if waiting for her answer. She wasn't even sure at this point what the question was? Ah, yes, he wanted to know what was on her mind. "If I told you what is on my mind, you may never forgive me for my thoughts." Had she said it out loud? Oh, she was becoming so bold with this man.

He grinned. "It may be possible I've got the same thoughts in my mind as well."

"Oh?"

He moved even closer. His mouth was an inch from hers. "I'm thinking now is probably not a good time to kiss you. Except my thoughts and my heart are not in agreement."

Marlene smiled. She knew exactly how he felt. She turned her head to see what Charlotte was doing. She was on the horse, her head leaning on the horse's mane, eyes closed, sleeping. The rocker had stopped moving. She wasn't looking at them. Perhaps a stolen kiss was possible.

When she turned back, Jack had the same idea. His mouth met hers in a stolen kiss she had wanted since she walked through the door tonight. Marlene put her arms around his neck, drawing him closer.

She felt his arms go around her waist, his big hands moving up and down her back. This was delicious and yet naughty, kissing a man in front of her sleeping daughter! What kind of woman was she?

Marlene pulled back. "I dare not, Jack. This isn't proper."

He let her go and nuzzled her cheek. "It may not be proper but it felt right. Don't you think so?"

"I do. Except, what if Charlotte was awake? What if she had woke up and saw us kissing?"

He laughed. "She'd jump up and down with glee and clap her hands."

Marlene shook her head and stood. "I'm sorry. We must get home."

He stood with her. "It's time we discussed our relationship, Marlene. I'm in turmoil of what to do. I think it is time we had a talk about us on Monday. There are things you should know about me."

Jack picked up a sleeping Charlotte and carried her home in his arms. When they got to her house, she opened the door and let him take her inside. As he went to leave, she placed a hand on his arm. "I agree we have to talk. I'm not ready yet to discuss everything about me. Not yet. I hope you understand."

He leaned over and kissed her on the cheek. As he left, Mack came up the steps. The two spoke outside for some time while Marlene settled Charlotte in bed.

She waited for Mack to get done talking outside. "Did you give him a hard time?"

"Of course not. I heard he was taking Clarissa to the Hart's farm tomorrow and wanted to make sure he had a buggy. He told me he already rented one from the livery. I am assuming you and Charlotte will be accompanying him?"

"Yes, he asked us both to go. Charlotte wants to make sure they will take good care of Clarissa."

He watched her with his all-knowing hawk eyes. "And you?"

"I like Jack's company."

"Just remember what I said."

"About his work? I have. Mack?"

He shook off his jacket, hanging it on the peg inside the door. When he looked at Marlene, he took her hand and sat her down. "What is it, sis? What's on your mind?"

She was trying to figure out her mind. Talking it out with Mack may be helpful as long as he gave her all the right answers. She smiled to herself. Wanting and getting the right answers was two completely different things. "First, thank you for bringing me here, Mack. It has literally saved my life. Dallas was not for me. I hated the big city, too much noise."

"Too many memories, I'm sure."

"That too. There's one thing you should know. Jack has brought me out of my shell. I feel alive for the first time in my life. I'm not hiding behind a cloak and hood. People are actually starting to get to know me. Even my life before all the horrible things with my husband Mark was lonely. He'd go for days and sometimes weeks at a time hunting or whatever it was he'd claim for that week. It got lonely in the cabin by the river."

"I'm sorry, sis. I wish you'd have told me. I'd have given him a good talking to."

She placed a hand on his arm. "He was too stubborn to take advice, even from you. Mark was determined until it killed him. I doubt the news of a child would have settled him down."

Marlene had realized all of this over the months after she had lost her husband. He had loved living off the land, leaving her at home so he had a woman to come home to. She had even asked him to take her along on his fishing and hunting excursions but he had refused. Said a woman's place was inside the house, not out on the frontier. It made her day to day life so lonely. When she realized she was having a baby, it was all she'd think about. Finally, someone else to love.

Then, when he died in the river and her brother had comforted her, she thought her life was over. Determined to stand on her own, she found out how foolish the idea was. Mack had gone chasing outlaws, which was his job as a Pinkerton. He vowed to help her but she didn't want to depend on him.

When she decided to become a mail-order bride to John Abbott, the real horror began. She shook her head. No sense in reminding herself what an utter fool she had been. The man was dead. Killed by the good folks of Mill Ridge. In a way, every single person in this town was a kindred spirit of some sort with each person trying to start over in a harsh world where it wasn't fair or easy.

She was glad Mack brought her here.

"Marlene, are you still with me?" Mack's voice drowned out the thoughts of that evil man. She took in a deep breath.

"I'm sorry. I started thinking about that day and -"

"You don't have to talk about it. Not if you don't want to."

She shook her head. "No, I don't want to. I actually want to put it all behind me. That's what I'm wanting to tell you. I have a lot of healing to do but I think Jack is the man I want to spend my life with. I trust him. I know you and some of the townsfolk are wondering who he is. I've seen his good heart. The way he treats Charlotte is astounding. The way he rescued a poor cow from an angry farmer shows me his heart. He has a good heart. Maybe he wants to get away from a past that is haunting him, too. You know, like the one that has haunted me since forever ago. I am ready to move on."

Her brother gave her a huge hug. "Best thing I've heard, sis. I guess I owe Jack a thank you. Did he ask you for your hand yet?"

"Not yet. I think he wants to but there is something on his mind. We're going to talk Monday when we go to supper together. Would you mind keeping Charlotte?"

"I'll be happy to. And, as the new deputy under Sheriff Nightingale, I'll be more than happy to reserve you a special place at the restaurant Monday. I usually stop there every morning."

Marlene laughed. "I suppose you will be taking a special treat to your favorite teacher?"

"It appears so."

"Oh, Mack, you are in love."

"I sure am. So are you. Do me a favor. I've sent a telegram the other day to inquire about Jack. Don't go getting salty on me. It is my duty as a brother to make sure you are going to be in safe hands."

"I understand. After all we've been through I knew you'd do so anyway. Let me know if you find anything out."

"I will. Goodnight, sis. I have an early rising. Jennie wants to go over our wedding plans."

Marlene eyes went wide! "I have been neglecting my brother and your future wife! Forgive me! The wedding is next Saturday and I still haven't a dress to wear."

Mack shook his head. "This wedding stuff is too much! Why, all this fuss for what, twenty minutes at the alter. I can think of better things to do with my time than fussing and carrying on about the perfect ceremony. We haven't even invited but a handful of people. She doesn't want a big fuss but it is turning out to be one in my book."

"Now, now, Mack! Every bride wants the perfect ceremony. I'll check in with Jennie tomorrow after we take Clarissa to the farm."

"She'll talk your ear off. I've been listening to it for the last few days."

Marlene listened as he ranted for the next ten minutes. Slowly closing her bedroom door, she giggled when Mack stopped all of a sudden realizing she was no longer listening.

In another minute his own door shut. She shook her head. There was no way she'd be fussing like that over a wedding. Nope. Not her.

Chapter 6

Marlene peeked out the window to see the buggy pull up in front of their house. Charlotte was jumping up and down, doing exactly what she was told not to do.

"Settle, now, young lady!" Marlene scolded as she passed by to answer the door. When she let Jack in he seemed in a happy mood this morning.

"Good morning!" he said, placing a quick kiss on her cheek. He whizzed by her and picked up Charlotte in one swoop. She giggled and kicked her feet. Her shiny patent shoes were going to get dirty on a farm.

"Charlotte, those shoes are not appropriate for a farm. Let's put on your older pair."

Jack waved a hand in the air. "No need. I think there is something in this sack for those feet!"

Charlotte squealed. "You brought me a present! Oh, Jack! I love you!"

Marlene's heart skipped a beat. She didn't want the child disappointed if Jack didn't want her. But every indication said he did. She'd soon know for sure. After their talk on Monday. What she had to tell him would determine if he stayed or not. She had thought about it all night long.

"If you are going to a farm, it's almost like being a cowboy or cowgirl, right?"

She nodded, her hair falling over her face. Charlotte brushed it back, the anticipation glowing in her eyes. "I want to be a cowgirl!"

"Then you will need a pair of cowgirl boots!" Jack reached in the bag and pulled out a pair of leather boots. "Let's see if these will fit."

It didn't take long for her to shake off her shoes and pull them on. They were a tiny bit big but Charlotte didn't care. She walked around the room, having a bit of difficulty but giving it her best shot. She placed her hands on her hips. "Now I need a cowgirl hat!"

"Then you best look in the other bag I brought."

Before long Charlotte was equipped with a new pair of boots and a wide brimmed hat. Marlene stuffed a sock in the tip of each boot so they fit better. She was ecstatic, running through the house, showing off. When she finally calmed down, she wore the biggest smile ever.

Marlene took a peek to see Jack watching her daughter with a proud look on his face. As if he wished she were his.

He tore his gaze away when he caught Marlene staring. A brow lifted and he grinned. "Didn't realize she'd be that excited."

"Charlotte is a happy child. She'll get excited about the simplest things. Except this is huge. Thank you, Jack."

He stood. "My pleasure. Guess we should be on our way. They are expecting us soon."

The ride to Grant and Annabelle's farm took longer than expected. They had attached a rope around Clarissa's neck and tied it to the back of the wagon. She wasn't too pleased to be taken from her little sanctuary or to have anything around her neck once again. "I understand how she feels," Marlene told him as they had to stop and urge her on several times.

Jack shrugged. "It won't be long, right up around this bend is the farm." Twenty minutes later they rounded the bend to find lush grass and fields galore. The farm set back from the road so they turned down the path towards the front yard. Little holes were scattered all over the area where they wanted to park the buggy in the front of the house.

"Look at those!" Charlotte pointed. Little prairie dogs peeked their heads out from a few of the holes. As soon as they realized they were being watched, they were gone.

"Don't go near them," Jack warned. "You don't know if they bite."

"They look so cute!"

Marlene had to laugh. Her daughter loved everyone and everything. She was so glad she had tried to shield her from the worst of life's troubles. Being here in Mill Ridge would give her daughter a wonderful place to grow up, away from the big city and horrible men.

A screen door slammed. Marlene looked up to see two little kids, one boy and a girl trailing across the wooden porch. "Over here!" They waved their little hands and arms.

A woman came out, young and beautiful with long golden hair, held back from her face but it's golden locks flowed down her back. She held a baby in her arms. "Don't walk across the prairie dog holes. Come around to this side!" she directed, waving towards the left.

They left Clarissa tied to the buggy and walked towards the welcoming family. Charlotte walked right up to the two children. "Hi. I'm Charlotte. I brought you my best friend, Clarissa."

The little girl smiled. "I'm Sadie and this is my brother John." She pointed to the baby in her mother's arms. "That's my baby sister Katie cutie pie. Hush, she's sleeping."

Charlotte gave Sadie a hug. "Do you want to see my cow?" She tugged on Sadie's sleeve and the two worked their way over to the buggy. The little boy followed behind.

Annabelle called out. "John, stay with your sister!" She welcomed Marlene with a huge smile. "Welcome to my madhouse. I'm Annabelle and you must be Marlene and Jack."

Her husband Grant came out from the barn, shaking hands and introducing himself. Soon, Jack and Grant went on their way back to the barn and to look at some new horses he recently purchased.

"Come inside, let's get some lemonade and we can sit on the porch while the little ones play."

Marlene helped her get glasses of lemonade for everyone, set them on a tray and went back outside. She held the baby for a time, cradling the infant in her arms. "She's beautiful," Marlene whispered, aching inside for another child of her own.

Right before she handed the infant back, Jack and Grant left the barn to take Clarissa to the pasture. She noticed his eyes on the baby, then on her own and his gaze softened. Was he wondering what it was like to have a child? Marlene was touched by the sincere look in his eyes.

"It's so nice to have you here, Marlene. It can be lonely living on a farm. Even with Elizabeth a half mile away, we're busy with our children and don't always get to visit as much as we'd like to. Grant said you would like to bring Charlotte every Saturday to visit with Clarissa?"

Although she didn't want to hand her over, the baby was searching for food. Annabelle settled the child on her lap, throwing a blanket over top and began to feed her. "If you don't mind, we'd like to bring her to see Clarissa. At least until she moves on and finds something else to love."

Annabelle laughed. "Ah yes, children do tend to do those things. Little John, who is named after my brother, had a kitten he thought he wanted to keep. When he realized he'd have to feed it milk every few hours, somehow it disappeared to the barn."

They laughed over that, then watched as Clarissa refused to move from the buggy. "Take off the rope from her neck!" Marlene shouted. When Jack nodded and did as she requested, the animal began to mosey around the yard. Between the two men and all three children, they finally got her inside the fenced area. The kids stood on the railing petting her as she tried to get used to her new home.

"Thank you for letting us keep her here. Jack's yard isn't big enough. Your brother was kind enough to suggest we let her go."

Annabelle smiled. "I can see how much everyone cares for her." She finished feeding the baby and handed her back to Marlene. "I made some sandwiches and set up a table alongside the house. Why don't we collect everyone and have something to eat."

"How nice of you," she told her, not minding at all if she had to tend to the baby while Annabelle got the food out. She followed her to the side of the house where a custom wood picnic table and benches were set up and a smaller table to set the food on.

Once Annabelle had all the food on the table, she went back out front and rang the bell attached to the front porch. The children came around the corner so fast, Marlene thought they were going to plough straight into the table. "Walk, ladies and gentleman!" At her tone, the children came to a screeching halt.

Annabelle came around the corner. "Have we washed up yet, children?"

The three looked back and forth at each other and ran for the well out front. Annabelle shook her head. "We go through this each and every day, sometimes they think I'm too mean. What they don't know is I love this life. Although it can get tedious, I would never trade it for anything."

Marlene didn't say much more after that. She was content to hold the baby while she slept, enjoying the talk between the men and the children's laughter. When it was time to clean up, she insisted on helping, placing the baby in her father's arms while she slept. As she went inside she noticed how Jack kept watching the sleeping baby.

Yes, he had what was called baby fever.

It made Marlene smile so wide she wasn't able to keep her happiness to herself.

Annabelle didn't know her well but she recognized something was going on. "Well, what has you so happy all of a sudden?"

Marlene hugged herself. "Jack. Did you see the way he kept staring at the baby?"

"I'm afraid I hadn't noticed." Annabelle began to put a few extra sandwiches in a small basket. "While you were busy staring at your man, the children asked if Charlotte may stay here and go to church with us in the morning. We can drop her off afterwards, or at church, whichever you think is best."

It wasn't too often Charlotte was away from her. Marlene bit at her bottom lip, trying not to seem nervous. She liked Annabelle and knew she'd take good care of her daughter. Maybe it was time to trust someone. The bad men were dead. She had made sure of it.

Annabelle paused. "Marlene, are you ill? You look pale."

She pulled herself together. "No, I'm fine. The thought of Charlotte away for a night has me worried. Not for her, I'm sure she'll be fine. It's me. I get anxious when she's not home." There, she told someone and didn't know why. She usually kept things like that to herself.

Annabelle gave her a hug. "Then it's high time you take a step back and do something kind for yourself. Here." Her new friend shoved a small basket in her hand. "I didn't see you eat much and Jack didn't eat but one sandwich, which is highly unusual for a working man. On your way home, there is a small stream down yonder, right before you get to the last bend at Mill Ridge. It's off the beaten path." She went to the drawer of her hutch and pulled out a small tablecloth. "Take this. You two need some time together. Grant and I go there sometimes. It is a perfect place to spend time with your loved one."

"Thank you." Marlene didn't know what else to say. They truly needed to talk and now more than anything, the opportunity was right in front of them. What she had to say really wasn't appropriate for Monday evening at supper. The small eatery in town may be packed with townsfolk and she didn't want anyone to hear what she was about to tell him. She was taking a risk. What she wanted to know from Jack, was he willing to risk his future on someone like her?

They waved as the buggy pulled away from the farm. Marlene saw how happy Charlotte was, playing with the other children and every now and again checking on Clarissa. "Notice how Clarissa is staying close to the fence?"

Jack nodded. "She will for a few days. When I first got her, she was afraid to move except for the times she opened the gate and wandered off, trying to get that bell off her neck. I am certain she'll be happy here once she gets used to the wide open fields."

"I believe you are right. It's a beautiful place."

"What do you have there?" He nodded to the basket on her lap.

Marlene wiggled her eyebrows. "A treat for the two of us. When you get to the last bend, there is a place to pull the buggy over and we can walk to the creek. Annabelle suggested it is a nice place to have a little picnic."

He frowned. "Didn't we just eat?"

"Jack. It's where Annabelle and Grant go to be alone."

He leaned in, smiling. "Ah, I see. Where I can kiss you without anyone mistakenly watching?"

"Possibly, however, you may not want to after we talk." It wasn't really proper to be alone with Jack and yet no one really went according to propriety in Mill Ridge. She trusted him and since no one in town said anything otherwise, she doubted there would be gossip. Unless someone came upon them at the creek, no one would know they ever stopped.

She said it in such a serious manner, a crease in Jack's brow was evident. "I doubt there is anything you tell me that would change my mind about how I feel about you."

His statement was bold. It gave her goosebumps knowing he cared for her and yet she had never told anyone the truth of that fateful night. Not even her brother. Yet, if she were to start a new life with this man, she had to be honest and tell him what happened. It was now or never.

"I believe the bend is right up there." She pointed to a place in the road where they were able to park. Jack helped her down and she took the basket along with the tablecloth as they walked through some tall grass to get to the creek.

The sound of water flowing and the coolness in the air gave hint they were close. A few trees hid the creek from view. They went around the trees to find a small grassy hill. "I believe this is the perfect spot for a picnic."

"Let me have the tablecloth." Jack opened it up and spread it on the ground, while Marlene set the basket down first, then herself. It took Jack a few minutes to join her as he was checking out the creek bank.

"What are you doing there, Jack?"

"Trying to see if this is a good fishing area. I wouldn't mind spending some serious time here."

"Well, did you find any fish?"

He came back and sat down beside her. "I didn't see anything from the bank. They probably heard us a mile away."

She giggled. "Do you think fish can hear you? That's silly."

He grinned. "It's what I heard. All my life I was told to stay quiet so the fish don't hear you."

Marlene had never heard such a story. "Are you possibly telling me a fish tale?" Her eyes crinkled with laughter when he threw his head back and laughed out loud.

She opened the basket and handed him a sandwich. "I believe it's turkey. Care for one?"

He nodded. "I'll never refuse food, that's for sure."

They munched on their food for a few minutes. Marlene had a hard time swallowing, let alone finishing. She waited until he was all done and took his hands. "We need to talk."

He frowned. "I thought we were going to do that on Monday night?"

"We have an opportunity to now and I doubt what I have to say is proper for a restaurant."

Her words caught his attention. "Marlene, I know there are things from your past. I don't care about them. I don't need to know everything. If it is too difficult to talk about, then let it rest with you."

She shook her head. "No, Jack. I can't. I'm not sure if I deserve any happiness."

"Of course you do. Probably more so than anyone I know of."

Her hands shook. He tried to still them when he took her soft hands in his. She looked directly in to his eyes. She had to see his true reaction when she spoke the next words. "I killed a man."

He stared. Jack tried to hide the surprised look on his face but she had already seen it. She closed her eyes for a moment. If he wanted to run, now was his chance.

She felt his warm breath so close to her. "Open your eyes and look at me."

She was afraid, so worried she would see disgust there. His fingers lifted her chin. "Come on, look at me."

She opened her eyes. He wasn't looking at her with disgust or horror or even disdain. His eyes were caring, loving, curious. "What happened?" he asked. "If you want to tell me, I'll listen."

She took a deep breath and her whole body shook. "I have to tell someone, it is eating me up alive. My husband died on the river, he drowned. I was alone living in a cabin outside of Dallas with a child on the way. My brother was always gone, he was a Pinkerton back then."

She stopped to catch her breath.

"Go on."

"I didn't want my brother to be forced to take care of us so I signed up through an ad to become a mail order bride with the stipulation I had a home for me and the child."

She was staring at the ground, trying to recall each dirty detail.

"Then what happened," he urged.

"John Abbott is what happened. He wanted slaves, not mail order brides. He had many women in rooms, locked away, trying to sell them to men of ill repute. John Abbott offered to buy my cabin except I never saw any money. Instead, I was sent to this terrible place until the baby was born, it was horrible. Men guarded the house day and night and we could not leave. There were several of us there, living in squander." She shivered at the memory. She had eaten better than any of the other women though. Abbott ordered the men to leave her be until after she had the baby. He said with her looks she'd bring a good price. That's when he grabbed her hair and kissed her with his rotten mouth. She made it through the kiss but had no idea what horror awaited her child.

She felt an arm slake around her shoulder. The warmth of Jack's body close to hers enabled her to continue her story. "After the baby was born, I fed her for a few days until one night, John Abbott ordered all of the women to be loaded on to this awful enclosed cart. It looked like a circus caravan. I was left there in the cabin with my child, alone with one guard."

She shivered. "I didn't think much about him or any of the others. Sometime during the night, I felt something was wrong. I went to reach for Charlotte, who had been sleeping in a small box with a blanket beside me on the floor but she was gone. I screamed, calling her name over and over again. The door to the cabin was unlocked and I stumbled outside.

The man who had stayed behind had my baby in his arms. He was moving closer to a wooded area and I followed behind, determined to find out where he was going with my child. I picked up a piece of wood from the porch, determined to fight him if he tried to hurt her. After about a mile, he stopped, unaware I was right behind. I placed a fist in my mouth so as not to cry out for my baby."

Marlene gasped for air, the memory too vivid, as if it were happening over again.

His gentle words directed her back. "It's fine, you're safe, Marlene. Look at me."

She did. This man was here, he wasn't going to hurt her or her daughter. She took in a few steady breaths. "I'm okay now."

"You sure? You can stop any time."

She shook her head. It was time to spill her guts. She didn't know what was going to happen to her after this. She supposed Mack would have to be told. Then the sheriff. She shivered again. Jack's arm tightened around her shoulder. "I looked at the ground in front of him, the loose dirt. It was, oh dear God, it was!" She put her hands over her face and sobbed. Jack held on, letting her be. She didn't dare look at him or she'd fall apart. "It was a grave."

"Marlene." His soft voice was what she needed to finish her story.

"A grave the size of my child. He was going to get rid of her. I don't know what came over me but I ran up behind him and with all the strength in me, I hit him over the head as hard as I could, hoping the moment he began to fall I'd snatch my child out of his arms."

The tears began. Jack tried again to wipe them away. She stilled his hands, squeezing them as if they were her life's blood. "He was so surprised, he stumbled and backed up a few steps. Then a look of surprise and horror came over him and he fell backwards into a ravine with my daughter in his arms." Her body shuddered. "I thought for sure I killed Charlotte along with him. I climbed down that ravine so fast I'm pretty sure I slid the whole way. My daughter was fine. She was encased in his arms, never one bump or bruise on her."

Jack pulled her closer and let out a sigh. "I'm so sorry, Marlene."

She swiped at more tears that fell. "That's not the whole story. I took my daughter and left that man there to die. He had called out to me to help him. Apparently he had fallen on a limb, a sharp point of it sticking through his leg. He wasn't able to move. I climbed up the ravine with my daughter and never looked back. I killed a man that night and I don't care. I'm glad he is dead. He tried to kill my daughter. I swear the Lord above woke me up from a dead sleep, otherwise, he'd have her buried in an unmarked grave."

"You've been through so much."

"I ran in to the woods like a posse was following me. We lived off the land for three weeks until my brother found me. I never told him about the man I left there to die. He doesn't know. I guess it's time to."

"You don't have to tell anyone else, Marlene. No one will blame you. That man created his own destiny. You were trying to save your daughter." Jack leaned in and kissed her softly.

"I have a heavy burden on my chest, Jack. My brother saved us, he gave me back my life. I owe it to him to tell him what I did."

"If you believe so, I'll be there when you want to tell him."

"Thank you. What if I go to jail? Jack, I don't know what I will do if that happens."

He helped her stand up. "We better get moving. Marlene, what you did was in self defense. Anyone will say so. To save your child like you did takes a lot of guts."

"Don't you see, Jack! You can't be with me if I'm labelled a murderer!"

Jack took her in his arms and held her there until every single tear dried up. "I'll be here for you, no matter what."

"You're too good for me, Jack."

He took both her hands in his, then slid to one knee. "Marlene, in spite of everything I find myself in love with you. I know marriage is a big risk but I do believe we both have what it takes to make a go of it. Will you marry me?"

Tears fell so hard she wasn't able to answer. "You, you still w-want to marry me after everything I told you?"

"Yes." Her heart filled with love.

When she nodded, he stood up and held her in his arms, placing a sweet kiss on her lips that stirred her insides. He still wanted her. "I think I'm falling for you too, Jack."

He gave her a knowing grin. "I suppose you are. I have to be as honest as you, although I can't tell you everything quite yet. Do you trust me?"

"I think so."

"Come on, let's walk back to the buggy." While they gathered everything up, he held her hand as they walked once more through the tall grass. "The town is right in thinking I'm holding something back. I am."

Marlene stopped to look at him. "For heaven's sake, Jack, what is it?"

"I need you to trust me. It's about what I do for a living. I can't tell you yet. Promise me you'll trust that I need a little time before I disclose my work to you."

Marlene gave him a curious look. "Are you an undercover man like my brother? A Pinkerton?"

He shook his head. "I'm afraid your brother would know if I was. No, sorry. Trust me, please. I have to speak with my boss first before I disclose anything."

She let him help her in the buggy. "I told you my story, Jack. The least you can do is promise me that before we get married, you'll let me in on your secret life?"

He gazed in to her eyes with so much adoration she almost told him she didn't need that reassurance.

"I promise," he said, then commenced to kiss her again, more deeply this time.

Chapter 7

Jack whipped the reins harder than he had intended to. After seeing Marlene to her door, he stopped by the saloon, a place he hardly ever entered but he needed desperately to let off some steam. He didn't want to go home yet. Not when his thoughts ran to wanting to strangle all those men who tried to hurt Charlotte, even if they were already dead and buried. "I'll take a sarsaparilla," he told the barkeep. "And a shot."

After a drink, he noticed the sheriff standing outside the saloon. Jack made his way through the doors. "Evening, Sheriff."

Nightingale nodded and tipped his hat. Jack was about to take a step off the porch when he noticed Marlene walking straight for the saloon. She pulled up her skirts to make it across without getting the hem of her dress muddy. "Sheriff! Sheriff! I'm turning myself in! Arrest me!" She dropped the hem of her skirts and held out her hands as if she were going to be cuffed right there in the middle of the street.

Nightingale pulled away from the post he had been leaning on. "Miss Marlene, what is this about? Lower your voice, you'll have everyone in town over here!" The sheriff tried to quiet her down but she was beside herself.

Marlene gave Jack a sad look. "I'm sorry, Jack. I can't live with myself any longer. Telling you made me realize I had to make this right."

He was almost right and he understood. "Sheriff. Can we go to your office? I think I can straighten this all up." Jack put an arm around Marlene and whispered in her ear. "Let's get off the street or everyone will be staring."

"I'm used to stares, Jack. Don't try to stop me. I listened to what you said but the more I got to thinking, I deserve to be put in jail for my sins."

Jack had enough. "If you don't lower your voice, everyone is going to be talking about how I hauled you over my shoulder to the sheriff's office. Now, do you want to walk there or have me carry you?"

She gave him a stare and then turned and led the way. Sheriff Nightingale shook his head and followed behind. "This is a first," he told Jack.

"Wait until you hear the whole story, then you'll understand."

"I can hear you two. Stop talking."

"I'm sorry, Marlene." Jack knew she was upset but he was pretty sure she wasn't going to be sent away for murder. She never even checked if the man had lived or died. He may well be alive for all she knew. Of course, since she had kept quiet about the whole mess, no one would have given her that information willingly.

When they were all seated inside the sheriff's office, Marlene insisted on placing herself in a jail cell. "It's for the best," she told the sheriff.

"I can't put you inside the jail until I know what happened."

Instead, she plunked down in a hard back chair on the opposite side of his desk in defeat. "Well I want to admit to killing a man."

He pushed his hat back. "What did you say?"

"It's true."

Jack held up his hand. "You don't know for sure if it is true. You are assuming."

The sheriff leaned in, staring Marlene straight in the eye. "Marlene, your brother told me what happened. He wanted me to understand what you went through so we can all protect you from anyone who ever comes to this town. Does your brother know about this man you allegedly killed?"

She shook her head. "I never told a soul. Until Jack."

The sheriff looked at him with a raised brow. "That part is true," Jack admitted.

Footsteps clunked on the outside porch right before the door swung open. Mack's large body came through the door. "Marlene, what's going on here?" His thunderous voice stopped everyone.

Marlene stayed calm. Her hands were twisted together in her lap but she held her own. Jack was proud of her.

"Mack, come take a seat," the sheriff offered.

"I'll stand. Sheriff, why do you have my sister in here and the whole town is gossiping that she murdered someone!"

"Wait, hold on. Mack, calm yourself." Nightingale turned to Marlene. "Tell your story. We're patient men." He leaned back while Marlene repeated everything she had told Jack earlier.

Her brother came to her side, knelt down and took her hands. "Marlene, do you mean to tell me all this time you kept this secret to yourself, thinking you killed someone?"

She nodded, tears of shame rolling down her cheeks. Jack wanted to go to her but knew this was a moment between brother and sister. Mack wrapped his arms around her and spoke softly. "My dear sister, no one was killed that night. We found an injured man a few days later but no one was dead. You didn't kill anyone."

"I didn't?" When the realization hit her, the look of relief on her face was priceless. Then she mumbled in to Mack's' shirt, "I probably should have killed the rotten, low-down excuse for a human being!"

Relief flooded through Jack. All this time she was living with the guilt she had killed someone. In his eyes it didn't matter if she had, the man had tried to murder her child. He'd do anything for his own child. He swiped at the sweat dripping from his brow. He'd do anything for Charlotte, even though she wasn't his. He hoped she would be someday though. Jack wanted to adopt her and give her a proper last name. He planned to talk to Marlene about it, but right now he had to fight his own demons before he took his bride-to-be to the alter.

Mack stayed to talk to the sheriff, while Jack offered to walk Marlene home.

When they got to her house, she insisted he sit with her awhile. "I don't much care what anyone thinks or speculates, we are soon to be married. I can't wait to tell Charlotte."

Jack obliged, spending the rest of the evening on the porch with her listening to how relieved her voice sounded. "You sound like a different person, Marlene."

She smiled. "Is that a good sign or a bad one?"

He leaned in. "It's wonderful. How long do we have to wait to marry?"

She shrugged. "I don't want to wait another day." Her hand snaked out and touched his face. He leaned into her warmth.

"How about next Saturday?" A female voice suggested out of the blue. Jack whipped his head around to see Mack and Miss Jennie standing there. They were on their evening stroll. Mack must've went straight to the boarding house to pick her up. He may have even walked by but neither of them had noticed. They were too busy staring into each other's eyes.

Marlene spoke up. "Next Saturday is your wedding, Jennie."

She nodded, a sly smile on her face and leaned forward. "And, it could be yours, too. Why can't we have a double wedding ceremony?"

Jack thought Marlene was going to cry. "I can't interfere with your ceremony!"

"Nonsense. Why wait? Everything is almost finished. You can help with the rest and we can truly be sisters! What do you say?"

Marlene stood and leaned over the porch rail to give Jennie a hug. "I would love to." She turned to Jack.

"Yes, let's do it." He smiled but inside he warred with himself. That gave him only a week to get his affairs in order. He noticed Mack watching him. Perhaps it was time to talk to someone in this town.

Maybe tomorrow.

"I'll stop by after school on Monday, Marlene, with all the details for Saturday. I'm so excited."

After Mack and Jennie left, Jack took her hands in his. "Are you sure you want to do this so fast?"

Marlene nodded. "Yes. I think one of the reasons Jennie suggested a double wedding is so we can get our homes in order. It works out perfectly. I can pack during the week and have our things at your house before Saturday. Then, after the ceremony, Jennie can move right in here while Charlotte and I move in to your house. It's a grand idea."

Jack gave her a sweet kiss on the cheek. "You ladies are very organized. Can't say I would be."

"Well, that's why you have me, Jack!"

"Would you like to take a walk?"

She snuggled closer on the bench seat. "I'd rather sit here with you and watch the night sky. Look!" A star shot across the sky, almost directly in front of them. "That's meant for us," she told him.

"I suppose it is." Jack had a lot of work to do. He prayed to that shooting star and his Lord Almighty, he'd do all the right things so Marlene would always be safe. If he brought harm to her because of his own doing, his life would be over. Mack would kill him, for certain.

<> <>

Marlene gave Charlotte a big hug in church the next day. She had made it through the night without worry, even though the child's presence was missed. "It sounds like you had a wonderful time," she told her daughter.

"Oh, mommie, it was so much fun."

"Hush, lower your voice, we are in church." Charlotte giggled and then took her mother's words serious when the preacher stood at the front. Her little legs flew back and forth during the sermon, accidentally kicking the underside of the pew. Marlene had to nudge her a few times. As soon as the service was over, Marlene knew to get her outside as soon as possible. The child was way too excited today to sit still any longer.

Jack met them out front. He gave her a look, the one that wanted to know if she gave Charlotte the good news yet. She shook her head. Now wasn't the time, not yet. She wanted Charlotte to settle down first before she sprang the news on her. The three walked to the side of the church where a pot luck social was set up in a grassy area. The three waited in line and helped themselves to some food before finding a spot beside the Grants. After they all ate, the children ran off to play a game with the other kids.

"Charlotte is a lovely young lady," Annabelle told her. "I'll forewarn you, I do believe next Saturday the children are making plans again."

Jack and Marlene looked at each other, realizing Saturday was the day to visit Clarissa.

"What is it?" Annabelle asked. "Is there something going on here you aren't telling me about?"

Marlene gave her a huge grin. "Next Saturday Mack and Jennie were having a quiet wedding at the church, nothing huge. Since Jack asked me to marry him yesterday after we left your farm, it has been decided to join them in a double wedding."

Annabelle screamed, throwing her arms around Marlene. "I'm so happy for you. It was the picnic at the creek, wasn't it?"

Marlene nodded, overwhelmed that someone was so excruciatingly happy for her. She valued Annabelle's friendship so much. "I may need some help getting a wedding dress."

"I'll help however I can. So will Elizabeth and I'll pass the word to the rest of the ladies in Mill Creek. You will have a bridal luncheon on Friday afternoon at two sharp."

Marlene looked worried. "I didn't tell Charlotte yet. I was waiting for the right time."

"I'll keep quiet until you tell her. But, do it today, I can't keep quiet for too long."

Another thought occurred to Marlene. "I don't think Jennie wanted a big deal made of the wedding. They were planning a quiet ceremony on Saturday. I don't think they even invited anyone else. I don't want to mix up her plans."

Annabelle stood up. "In that case, it's time to talk to Miss Jennie. No one gets away with sneaking around Mill Ridge. She is an integral part of the town and therefore she will also be invited to the bridal luncheon if I have to drag her there myself." She turned and marched over to where Jennie and Mack were watching the children.

Jack whistled. "She is vocal. I heard she can be a handful. Her husband says it all the time."

Marlene laughed. "The two are a match made in heaven, that's what I saw. I believe she has to be tough to keep her husband in line. He was a loner and a Texas Ranger before they met, so I understand."

Jack nuzzled her cheek. "Are you going to keep me in line?"

"If you are naughty, yes."

They both burst out laughing. Some others at the table looked their way, but Marlene didn't care. She had been quiet for far too long. It was time to enjoy her life. Jack made her laugh and smile whenever she was with him.

On the way home, Charlotte took both their hands and skipped down the street in between the two. It was hard for them to keep up. The girl had an enormous amount of energy. "My goodness, Charlotte. Slow down or you'll wear us out!"

Jack roared with laughter. Which made Marlene burst out giggling and then Charlotte began to jump up and down more, her giggles heard above everyone. When they all sobered up, Marlene thought it was as good a time as any to speak with Charlotte.

"How about if the three of us sit on the porch and watch the world go by?"

"Can we, Mommie? Can we have some lemonade?"

"I'll go get some but you have to promise me to settle down now."

She placed her hand over her little heart and gave a big smile. "I do."

Jack helped get Charlotte settled while Marlene went for the drinks. She brought them out on a tray. Jack stood and took the tray, waiting until she was settled before handing her a drink.

Marlene took a deep breath. She was almost certain Charlotte would be happy about the news and yet it still made her nervous. It had only been the two of them for five long years. "Charlotte, Jack and I have some news."

Her little cheeks pinked as she smiled. "Is Jack going to be my daddy?"

Marlene wanted to see Jack's reaction. His face softened and he nodded. "If you will have me as your daddy, young lady, then yes."

She tilted her little head. "Are you going to marry my mommie?"

Jack smiled. "Yes, as long as it's fine with you."

Charlotte nodded, her little curls starting to bounce, along with the rest of her. Then she stopped. "Mommie, does this mean we get to live at Jack's house?"

Marlene smiled. "Yes, honey, we will."

Her little eyes got so wide. "I get to ride the wooden horsey any time I want?"

"Well, that depends if you behave and do your chores."

"I like chores."

"Well, then you will have no trouble."

"Will we get to see Clarissa every Saturday?"

"Yes, dear, we'll go as a family and maybe even stop and have a picnic along the way."

She clapped her little hands together, forgetting she held a drink in her hand. The lemonade splashed over the brim of the glass.

Marlene waited for the next question.

"Mommie?"

"Yes, dear?"

Can I invite John and Sadie to my new house?"

Marlene looked to Jack. She didn't want to overstep her bounds right away. He had been a bachelor up until now. Having her and Charlotte would take some adjusting to. "How about if we wait until we are settled to decide that. We'll have to discuss overnight guests with Jack."

Charlotte nodded and turned to Jack. She didn't say a word, her little chin shot up in the air, and her little brows were raised up. When he looked at her serious expression, Jack grinned. "I'm sure we can make arrangements. How about if we get through the wedding next Saturday first?"

"We're getting married on Saturday! I can't wait! I'll have a new daddy by Saturday!"

"Settle down, young lady. Now, let's watch the stars, it's starting to get dark out. Look at that cluster up there." Marlene knew how to distract her daughter, she loved watching the sky. After awhile, she leaned against Marlene, her little eyelids drooping.

Jack scooped her up in his arms as Marlene opened the door. After she got the child tucked in to bed, Marlene came back outside to see Jack standing on the porch, staring at the sky. "Everything okay, Jack?"

"Everything is fine." He turned to smile but she noticed a worried look on his face. Perhaps he was having regrets. Second thoughts? He held out an arm and she slipped in beside him. They stood there for the longest time before she heard him let out a long sigh. "I better go."

She needed to know they were making the right decision. "Jack? Are you certain you want to marry me on Saturday?"

He stared down at her then encased her cheeks in the palms of his hands. "I would marry you tonight if it were possible," he told her in that gravely voice of his.

"That's all I needed to know," she told him, before raising her mouth to his in a slow, deep kiss.

Saturday couldn't come any sooner.

Chapter 8

Jack had sent the telegram first thing in the morning. The telegraph office was closed and he hadn't heard anything yet. It was Monday evening and he was about to pick up Marlene for their supper date. Not knowing what his boss thought of his impromptu idea made him nervous. He had told his Publisher he was getting married on Saturday and needed it all taken care of by then.

Surprised at no response, he decided to have a nice supper with Marlene and send another telegram in the morning. Once he was reassured everything was taken care of, he'd tell his bride-to-be the truth of the matter. It had been weighing heavily on his chest these past few days. He didn't want to start their new life together with any secrets.

She had been honest with him.

Marlene had every right to know the truth about him.

Not yet, though. Not until it was taken care of.

He knocked on her door and adjusted his jacket as he waited for it to open. A little face peeked out. "Hello, Charlotte. I've come to take your mother to supper."

The door opened wide. "Hello, Jack. I told everyone in school today that you are going to be my new daddy." He noticed she wasn't smiling like she always does. He bent down on one knee.

"What's wrong, Charlotte?"

She sniffed, her little face looking at the ground. "One of the boys said I was telling a tall tale and then everyone laughed at me."

He reached out and picked her up, holding her up to meet his gaze. "Now, Charlotte. We're going to make sure there's no misconception about me being your daddy. I'm coming to school tomorrow and tell them myself!"

Her eyes got huge! "You will?"

"I sure will and I'll tell you what else. If your mommie doesn't mind, instead of staying here with your uncle, why don't you come along with us to supper and I'll tell everyone in the restaurant, too! Soon, the whole town will know I'm going to be your daddy!"

Charlotte slid out of his arms and ran in to get her mother. Jack wanted to find the kid that made fun of her and have a talking to the boy's father but he knew that was overdoing things. He had to be careful how he approached this new role. He didn't want to advocate violence and yet the boy was upsetting with his soon-to-be-daughter.

Marlene was led outside by little Charlotte in the lead. Jack had waited on the porch, a bit nervous. He turned. "My two favorite ladies."

Marlene gave him a huge smile. She looked relieved. "Thank you for inviting Charlotte along. She was quite distressed to the point I was afraid of canceling our supper."

"No need. Are you two ladies ready to go for supper?" He held out an arm for each of them. Charlotte's hand reached up for his. This child was looking up at him with all the trust in the world. He wasn't about to let a bully discourage her or intimidate her. She would learn to stand up for herself and he'd help. After all, as her soon-to-be father, it was the proper thing to do.

The line was long at the restaurant this evening. It was a rather small building but the only one in Mill Ridge to get a decent supper. Besides, the saloon wasn't proper for his two ladies. He tried to keep Charlotte entertained by making funny faces behind her mother's back but each time he did, Marlene turned around and caught him, causing Charlotte to giggle even more. The others in line laughed along until two or three other townsfolk began to play, too.

When they were seated after a twenty minute wait, Jack quickly ordered the daily special for everyone and a glass of fresh milk for Charlotte. While they waited for the food, he stood up, a knife in one hand and a glass in the other. He commenced to tap the glass. "May I have everyone's attention, please!"

The crowd settled after a moment. Everyone seemed curious now as all eyes were on him. "I have an announcement to make. Make sure to spread the word and tell everyone Marlene and I are getting married this Saturday!"

The crowd clapped and whistled. A few shouts were heard. He tapped the glass again. "I'd also like to announce and you can tell every single person in the town that I am proud to call Miss Charlotte, Marlene's five year old daughter, my own as well. I will be her daddy!"

Charlotte clapped like nobody's business. Her smile was so wide and she smiled for so long Jack thought she'd never stop. When the food arrived, he sat down at the table. Marlene gave him a grateful look while the child dug into her food. She only looked up when her mother coughed several times.

"Charlotte," Marlene scolded. "Take my hand, please."

They said prayers and it didn't take Charlotte long to finish her food. "Are you done already, young lady? How about some dessert."

She shook her head. "No. I want to go home to bed so tomorrow hurries up."

Marlene leaned in closer to discuss her manners. His heart swelled watching the two of them. Even though he had a deadline to meet before their wedding, he wasn't about to disappoint her. He'd walk in to the school tomorrow and show them she was telling the truth. No one was going to laugh at her again. It was worth it to see the smile on her face. She trusted him completely. That's what Jack took home with him that night. The two women who meant the world to him. Their beautiful smiles. It was worth everything he was about to do.

<> <>

An oversized buggy rode through the center of town late Thursday evening. Marlene and Jack were taking their evening stroll, with Charlotte in the middle. It had been a hectic week trying to get ready for Saturday's ceremony. "This is nice," Marlene said out loud. "It's been quite a fast-paced week, hasn't it?"

Jack agreed. "It has, but you are right. This is a nice walk. I'm enjoying our stroll. I hope we continue it even after we are married."

Charlotte agreed too. "I hope you don't leave me behind."

"Never, darling. You can come, too."

"Do I get to come to the bride party tomorrow?"

"I believe so. The whole class will be escorting Miss Jennie to the Jenning's Farm. It's going to be quite the luncheon. Elizabeth and Annabelle have invited some of the ladies from Wichita Falls to join in the festivities." Her wedding gown was almost finished. She didn't know how these ladies were going to pull it off but they swore it would be done in time. Elizabeth had an older gown she donated, while Annabelle had lace and one of the other ladies donated long white gloves. They planned to show her the final details tomorrow at the luncheon.

"It sounds like something I need to stay away from," Jack joked.

Marlene grinned. "I believe you'll be plenty busy yourself. According to Mack, the men have something planned for the two of you."

Jack groaned. "I do have plenty of work to keep me busy."

"Look at that horsey!"

The buggy had stopped in the middle of the street. All eyes were on it when the door popped open and a fancy dressed fellow worked his way out of the enclosed carriage. Not too many people used them much. Residents usually had to haul merchandise around and a wagon or open buggy was much easier.

Jack grinned. "I'll be! This is better than a telegram!"

The man picked up a small carpetbag and walked towards Jack. "I'll say this is in a remote area! Took me four days by train, and a buggy to get here."

Marlene watched as the two shook hands. Jack turned. "Marlene, this is my boss, Mr. Beadle. I believe he decided to attend our wedding."

She tried not to show surprise. This was the first he spoke about what he did for a living. "Hello, Mr. Beadle. How are you?" The man shook her hand with a firm grip.

Jack motioned for Charlotte to come forward. She walked slowly as if the man may bring her harm. "This is Charlotte. I am going to be her Daddy."

Charlotte's eyes crinkled as she nodded, no longer scared. "Hello. Do you know what Jack did the other day?"

Mr. Beadle furrowed his brows. "What did Jack do?" He looked on in amusement, first at Jack, then Charlotte.

"Well, he came to my school and told everyone he was going to be my daddy come Saturday morning. Now, no one will ever make fun of me again."

"Is that a fact?"

Charlotte nodded, crossing her hands across her waist. "Yes, sir, that is a fact."

They all laughed.

It looked like Mr. Beadle and Jack had business to attend to. Marlene didn't want to hold them up. "If you don't mind Jack, we'll be getting on home. Nice to meet you, Mr. Beadle."

Jack spoke to his guest and followed Marlene and Charlotte home, giving them both a hug before hurrying back to where Mr. Beadle stood along the side of the street waiting. Marlene tried to picture what kind of business the man was in but didn't have any idea.

Sooner or later, Jack would fill her in. She hoped. He asked her to trust him and she did.

Didn't she?

<><>

"A toast to the brides!"

"Here! Here!" The yard was filled with almost every woman in Mill Ridge and some of the ladies from Wichita Falls as well. It wasn't often they had a bridal luncheon. Elizabeth and Annabelle knew everyone, it seemed. Marlene was surprised she wasn't getting anxious with so many people there. Even the school children were here for the festivities.

Clarissa pushed her big body against the wooden fence loving all the attention. Charlotte was in her glory explaining the animal's story and how she got to live on the farm. Marlene was in heaven. This was a perfect end to a hectic week.

"Tomorrow we'll be married, Jennie."

Jennie closed her eyes. "I can't wait."

"Same here."

"Marlene, please stand up."

Marlene looked around. All eyes were on her. She didn't like being the center of attention.

"Come on now. We have your wedding dress ready for you."

Marlene was so nervous. She stood.

"Close your eyes."

She closed her eyes.

"No peeking," someone teased as they all laughed. Feet shuffled around until it there was a silence with some tiny oohs and ahhs filtered across the yard.

"Now open your eyes."

Marlene blinked at first, then blinked again. When her eyes steadied, she gasped. "It's beautiful," she whispered. Tears filled her eyes and she knew any moment they'd splash over onto her cheeks.

Someone handed her a handkerchief. "How did you know this is my favorite color?"

"We didn't but it seemed to fit you perfectly." Elizabeth Holloway pulled her shoulders back. "You both will be perfect brides tomorrow. We can't wait."

"Here! Here!" The crowd clapped and shouted again. Marlene never felt more loved than she did right then. Her life was almost too perfect, and while it was, she was going to eat this up. There had been too many dark and lonely days in her past.

"Thank you, everyone. I'm so grateful for each one of you."

"Our pleasure. It's what life in our small town is all about. We stick together here. You'll always find a friend at any given time."

"Here! Here!" Marlene said, raising her own glass in the air. A town filled with new friends and faces. Her sanctuary had now become her home.

All of these people were a part of her life now.

She smiled at Charlotte as the little girl waved to her. Marlene sighed. Tomorrow she'd be Mrs. Jack Fergenson. Wife of a well, she didn't even know what he did for a living. He promised to tell her. Tonight was his last chance to see her before the wedding.

Should she worry?

Was he going to tell her or ask her to trust him again?

It seemed strange his boss would travel so far to see him married. Was there something more to this than meets the eye?

What if he was doing something illegal or horrible to hurt others? Why did she even think that way? He was such a nice man. Maybe he was worried no one would like him if he disclosed his job. With the appearance of his boss here, she hoped he would explain things.

Later that afternoon when they got home, her mind was nearing exhaustion from wondering about the wedding tomorrow, Jack's work and his obligation to tell her. She tried to close her eyes several times but it seemed impossible to rest. Her mind didn't want to stop the questions.

Instead, she gazed at the beautiful wedding gown hanging from a hook on the wall. The ladies all worked on it to her surprise. It turned out so beautiful she wondered if she was deserving of such a dress. It was a lavender gown that would hug her shoulders with white chiffon and a train of soft tulle that fell from the waist to flare out behind. She was so anxious and yet terrified at the same time.

Was this what it was like for all brides? Maybe Jennie had been right to want a small, no-nonsense wedding. Except Elizabeth and Annabelle gave her a good talking to and changed Jennie's mind. The whole town was officially invited to the wedding tomorrow.

Marlene felt herself starting to get anxious. Even though she had no reason to, she didn't know if she deserved so much happiness all in one shot.

The sound of someone knocking on the door distracted her distracting thoughts. Marlene hurried to answer to find Jack standing there, a small bunch of daisies in his hand. He held them out to her.

She motioned for Jack to come inside while she placed the flowers in a vase with water. She motioned for him to keep quiet since Charlotte had fallen asleep after all the festivities. "Let's go outside on the porch," she whispered after setting the vase on the table. "I'll get us something to drink."

Jack nodded and waited while she made some warm tea for the two of them. She wasn't even sure if he liked tea. What did she really know about her husband-to-be? Taking a deep breath, Marlene realized they had quite a bit of talking to do this evening before they were married tomorrow.

He must feel the same way, she thought. When she sat on the porch, he moved to the rocking chair instead of sitting on the bench beside her. Why was that? she wondered.

"Jack, why are you sitting so far away?"

He didn't look at her. "I have to disclose some things, Marlene. It's easier from here."

"Will I be upset with you?"

"I hope not."

"Then, come sit with me on the bench. I want to hold your hand while you tell me this news."

Jack tilted his head and looked at her as if seeing her for the first time. He stood, moved to the bench and held out his hand. A shudder went through him. She felt it. Was this bad news?

He turned to look at her, his hazel eyes intense. "Marlene, I'm sorry if I never disclosed my line of work to you before. I've kept it to myself to keep you safe."

She frowned. "Safe? Whatever do you mean, Jack?"

"I am a writer of dime novels."

It occurred to her the dime novel she had held in her hand that day was his work. That was why he had looked so dismayed. He had been afraid she found out. "The author's name was J. Fergy?"

He nodded. "I write under a nom de plume. I'll admit when I saw you holding the book, it scared the daylights out of me. The memory in my head was so dark and horrible I backed away from you that night. I want to apologize."

"No need." She squeezed his hand, although he was clinging to her own with a firm grip. "Why hide it, Jack? I assume Mr. Beadle is your publisher then?"

"He is." Jack ran his other hand through his hair, taking in a huge breath of air. "I've become quite a famous writer of dime novels by the pseudonym of J. Fergy. I did some signings and public affairs in the city and met some of my biggest fans. There was one, a woman who would not stop pestering me. She even found out my real name and where I lived and came calling. I had to send her away several times. There was an incident in public where the police had to be called over. She was getting a crazed look in her eyes, which was not normal. My fans were relentless adventurers, even young boys and teens who loved the call of the west in my work. She was unusual and a threat."

"How terrible. I can't imagine being so famous!" Marlene was starting to realize Jack had gone through his own trauma.

"It gets much worse." He hung his head and stared at the ground for a few moments. He seemed to have trouble with his next words. "I had gone to a book signing with my editor that afternoon. When I returned home, my front door was ajar. My sister Janey had come for a visit. She loved to see the city lights and shows. She had not been feeling well. When I went inside she had been murdered. Stabbed to death by the woman who had been stalking my career." Jack let out a guttural sob, a giant, raspy sob that made his whole body shudder.

Marlene stood up and wrapped her arms around his shoulders. "I'm so sorry, Jack."

He stayed in her embrace until he got his voice back. "Janey was sixteen years old. She was in my care and I failed her. My parents blamed me, you know. They haven't spoken one word to me since I had to tell them what happened."

"It wasn't your fault. The woman was demented."

"She was. They sent her to Blackwell's Island, a lunatic asylum. My work as a writer almost came to a standstill after the trial until my boss told me to put that anger in my books. So I did and they even got more popular. I hated the big city by then and wanted to get away. When a friend of mine told me about his uncle's demise here in Mill Ridge, I bought the house by proxy and left the city for good."

"You mean to tell me you didn't even know where you were heading to?"

He shook his head. "I had no clue except it was a small town without a railroad. They claimed it was growing bigger but it sounded like heaven to me. My boss agreed to send him a manuscript each Friday so it didn't interrupt my work schedule."

"It was nice of him to come to your wedding."

"He came because I wrote to him about killing off J. Fergy."

"What? Stop writing?"

"No, that's not my intention. I'll always write. It's in my blood. I don't know what else to do with my life if I didn't write. I vowed never to put anyone else in direct harm. It's why I hesitated asking you to be my wife at first. If anything happened to you or Charlotte from one of my fans, it would truly be my end."

Marlene placed a kiss on his mouth. He clung to her, clearly distressed but when he kissed her back with all of his emotions, it was almost too much for Marlene. She pulled away, taking his face in her hands. "Jack. Nothing will happen to us. You're known here as Jack Fergenson. No one will ever know who you are."

"That crazy woman in New York followed me and found out who I was. I was hoping to start over here, it's why I didn't disclose my work to anyone in this town. I'll never do any book signings or gatherings again. Do you realize if anyone learns where I live, anything can happen. I can't lose anyone else I love."

Marlene held him for the longest time. "Jack, what will you do now as far as a writing career if you kill off your non de plume?"

"I'll write under another name. My boss is working on that right now. He is going to announce the death of J. Fergy before the day is over via telegram. It will get to the front pages of all the newspapers immediately. By the time we marry tomorrow, my fictitious name is dead and you will stay safe. It's all I wanted and I'm sorry I waited this long to talk to you. I had to make sure it was guaranteed you would always be safe first. I can't lose you, Marlene."

"Oh, Jack!" Their lips came together in a sweet kiss, so sincere it almost made Marlene cry.

"I have to ask you to keep what you heard tonight to yourself, Marlene. I can't risk it getting out."

"There are people who are suspicious of what you do, Jack. We have to give people something. Perhaps you can introduce your boss. Plus, everyone knows you send a package each Friday and they are curious."

"I thought about telling your brother. He gives me a steady look every time we are alone in the same room. I know he wants to ask me but has not yet. I'm not sure what I'll tell him."

"The truth, Jack. You can trust my brother."

"I'm afraid to. Truly, I am."

"I promise to say nothing to anyone right now. But, sooner or later, I will feel inclined to explain to my brother. I need you to try to trust more people. Not everyone is crazed. There are people here who love you. Look at me. I thought I was alone in the world. Now I have so many people who love me I can't take it all in."

Jack sighed. "In time, perhaps."

Marlene hadn't noticed the dark figure until she looked up to see her brother standing there.

Mack Everett frowned. "No need to explain things to me, Jack. I already know."

Jack's head whipped around. He stood. "How?"

"I have my ways."

"He was a Pinkerton, Jack. He always gets to the bottom of things. He isn't going to let me marry someone of ill repute. I told him you weren't, but he had to find out for himself."

Mack leaned against the rail, close to where Jack stood on the porch. "Jack, I'm a bit disappointed that you didn't discuss this with the sheriff when you first came to town. It not only put my sister in danger, but the whole town as well."

Jack gritted his teeth. "I know. I had heard Mill Ridge was a place where no one cared about your past. I didn't think it mattered until I met Marlene. I've taken steps to keep her safe."

"You swear?"

"Yes. J. Fergy, well-known dime novelist will be dead by morning."

"Good idea. I suppose you'll keep writing?"

"Yes, under a new name."

"Make sure to tell me what that name will be."

"Why's that, Mack?"

Mack smiled and came up on the porch. He turned before going inside. "I enjoy those dime novels, Jack. I want to see what happens next."

Marlene nudged Jack and gave him a big smile. "See, I told you he won't care. Now, he'll make sure no one ever bothers you again. It's best to let the sheriff know, too. Perhaps you can talk to him after the wedding tomorrow."

Mack shook his head. "No can do."

"Why not?"

"I'll be spending the whole day with my new wife. She gets all my attention tomorrow."

"What about your boss? He is here to visit."

"He will be heading out the moment the wedding is over. He spends months at a time at a retreat in Colorado. He sneezes and coughs a lot, it does his lungs good."

"Annabelle is taking Charlotte with them to the farm tomorrow. We'll have the whole evening and overnight to celebrate our wedding."

"I know. I plan to celebrate with the woman I love."

"Kiss me, Jack. Kiss me good."

He didn't hesitate this time.

Chapter 9

Tears rolled down her face as she walked towards her husband-to-be. The church was filled to capacity, with some residents standing. This double wedding had everyone wearing their Sunday best to attend. She doubted there was anyone left home alone today. The street outside the church was clogged with horse and buggy's from as far away as Wichita Falls. Everyone loved weddings and parties, it seemed.

Jennie walked beside her in a beautiful white gown. The two smiled at each other through the veil over their faces. "Sisters forever," Jennie whispered.

Marlene was too choked up to speak so she gave her a nod. They finished their walk down the aisle as everyone in church watched. There were so many sets of eyes on the brides, Marlene was afraid she'd start to shake. When she saw Jack standing there beside her brother, with the reverend behind them, she let out a sigh of relief. Taking this walk down the aisle was nothing compared to her last five years. Especially when a man like Jack was waiting to make her his wife.

She'd take this walk any day.

Jack leaned over and whispered in her ear. "You look beautiful."

"And you, dear Jack, look so handsome."

"May I have your attention please. Let's begin with this special chapter of Corinthians," the reverend said, his voice rising above the rumble of soft voices still talking. Marlene didn't hear a word of what was said. She dared a peek at Jack, who stared at her, his intense eyes filled with adornment. She hoped to get through this day without a panic attack. Her heart was ready to burst wide open!

Twenty minutes later the good reverend announced them husband and wife, along with Mack and Jennie. The crowd cheered and clapped like nobody's business. She heard the buzzing in her ears but she had eyes only for her husband, who was moving towards her to seal the deal with a kiss.

"I love you, Marlene," he told her right before his mouth came down on hers in a breathless kiss that almost made her faint.

She stepped back when he released her. "My goodness gracious, husband! That was some kiss!"

"There's plenty more where that came from." He gave her a wink, turned to the crowd and smiled so wide she thought his face would crack apart. Instead of continuing to worry, Marlene gave in and raised her hand in the air, holding the bouquet of flowers over her head. She let her head fall back and looked up. *Thank you, my Lord. I've been through the darkest hour and now you've led me to the brightest light. I'm grateful for my blessings.*

"Hey, Mrs. Fergenson. You alright?"

She giggled. "Yes, Mr. Fergenson. I'm ready to go home."

He nodded. "I agree but we're not done yet. The townsfolk have tables lined up outside for a reception and a wedding cake. There's Charlotte. I think she wants to say goodbye."

Charlotte ran to her. Even though she was wearing a beautiful gown, Marlene reached down and scooped her daughter up in her arms. It didn't matter if her little shoes clung to the gown when she wrapped her legs around Marlene's waist. They both had been down a long, tiring road to get to this point. She had tried to keep Charlotte's life as normal as possible, even when she was in her non-speaking mode. Even though kids made fun of her for not having a real daddy, at least now she'd have a loving home. And a real daddy.

"I'm going to stay at the farm tonight. Clarissa misses me. I'll see you tomorrow at church mommie. I love you." Marlene held her for the longest time until Charlotte wiggled to get free. She let her down and watched as her five year old jumped up to have Jack catch her in his arms. She flung her little arms around his neck. "I love you, daddy. I can call you daddy, now. You are married to my mommie."

"I love you too, Charlotte."

Marlene thought Jack was going to cry but he maintained his composure the whole time. After Charlotte left with the Jennings family, Jack turned to her. "I think I'm done for. That daughter of yours completely took me off guard."

She shook her head. "You haven't seen anything yet. Let's go socialize with the guests so we can go home." All week long they had moved what furniture she had to Jack's house. Jennie had done the same thing but she didn't have much except for a few suitcases of clothes and a special family book she placed on the mantle. When Charlotte came home on Sunday, she'd be going home to Jack's house. Their new house.

It was the start of a new life. One she was going to embrace.

Everyone was outside crowded around the table where the wedding cake sat on. Glasses were raised and they were just about to cut the cake when Mr. Beadle cried out. "Ack! Here comes trouble."

Everyone in the crowd, including Jack and Marlene, looked at the buggy coming down the street, trying to park amongst the many there.

Jack spoke up first. "Who is that?"

"That's Frank Wetling. He's a dog-gone reporter trying to make himself famous. I'm afraid he must've followed me here, Jack. I've sent the telegram we talked about but if he sees you here, it won't matter much. He'll be able to dispute my words."

The crowd was listening. "We can run him off," one of the older citizens shouted before knowing why.

"No, can't do that, he'd become suspicious," Beadle replied.

Jack sighed. He held up his hands for quiet. "I'm going to be honest with all of you. Some of you wondered what I do for a living, well, I'll tell you. I write dime novels by the name of J. Fergy. Except as of today, we killed off the fictitious name J. Fergy. My boss here, Mr. Beadle just sent notice of J. Fergy's death. But this feller," he pointed to the man trying to park the buggy, " he is a reporter trying to find my identity. I'm sorry, folks, I had to keep quiet about my work. Now, I realize you are all my family and I should've told you in the first place."

"Darn tootin' we are and we ain't gonna let some young buck find out any of Mill Ridge's secrets. Let's all make a pack right now, folks. No one will ever know who this man is!"

"Here! Here!" One after another shouted out until everyone was calling out. Most of them didn't care, all they wanted was to make sure one of their own was protected.

Marlene saw the reporter find a spot to park his buggy. "Has he ever seen you before, Jack?"

"I'm not sure. If he poked around in the city, he may have an idea of what I look like."

"We better get out of here, Jack. Here he comes."

The crowd hid the newly married couple by forming a wall until they were able to sneak alongside the church and run down one of the side alleys. Marlene held on to Jack's hand as he took the lead. "I hope Charlotte got away in time!"

"She did. I saw Grant get everyone in his wagon and they took off."

"Good. I'd hate to be told on by my own child. She won't understand, she's too young."

"Not going to happen. Here, turn up this way." They ran through a few yards and were even chased by some stray chickens until they made it to Jack's house. He held open the gate, closing it after her. He wrapped his arms around her waist and lifted her up in his arms. She giggled like a young school girl.

Jack strolled up the walkway, taking the two steps to his porch and kicked open the front door. He grinned down at Marlene. "Welcome home, Mrs. Fergenson."

And he took her over the threshold.

Marlene stretched the next morning, realizing how wonderful it was to be alive and well. The sun shone bright through the upstairs window. She was truly a bride, for the second time. Yet, it felt like the first time. Her first husband never treated her like a precious jewel, carefully considering her feelings in every aspect of their time together.

She grinned.

"Come join me," her husband told her.

She peeked out from under the covers to find him sitting by a large window. There was a small table where two cups of coffee sat. She wrapped the sheet around her and moved to the chair he had pulled out for her. "This is a nice view. You can practically see the whole main street from here."

He kissed her gently on the mouth. "I've been quite entertained this morning. Usually the streets are still on a Sunday morning except for a few people here and there. Not today. Can't say I know what's going on."

A tapping at the front door caused Marlene to jump up. "I better get dressed."

He shook his head. "I forbid it, my lady."

Marlene's eyes widened. "You can't forbid me to get dressed!"

"I am your husband and I say no." He nuzzled her neck and made her giggle. "I'll be right back as soon as I get rid of this intruder. We have much work to do."

She laughed to herself when he left in his bare feet. Whoever was intruding must not be aware of their wedding yesterday. The whole town had been there and knew about it. Her thoughts went to her daughter. Right away, she thought about Charlotte. What if something happened?

She was about to run to the top of the stairs to listen when she heard her brother's voice. With a sigh of relief, Marlene went back inside the room until Jack returned. If something happened, Mack would've already called out to her. She had no doubt.

When Jack returned he had a devil-may-care look on his face.

"What is it?" She waited until he sat back down and slid on his lap.

He wrapped both arms around her waist and pulled her close. "Seems the town of Mill Ridge is going to be in mourning today."

"Oh? What happened?"

"The town is holding a public funeral for the famous writer J. Fergy. Can you believe it?"

"Are you serious?" Marlene didn't know whether to laugh or frown. "Why is this a good thing?"

"Your brother stopped by to tell me that last night after we snuck out of the reception, this reporter began to ask everyone questions about J. Fergy. Everyone was answering the best they can and then someone from the crowd shouted out that we were having the funeral this morning. The man was going to leave, go back to Wichita Falls and hook up on the next train. That loud mouth ruined things. Even so, the town is pulling together to convince him Fergy is dead. We're burying him today at eleven in the morning."

Marlene began to laugh. "Can we go?"

"To the funeral?"

"Yes. You can't go as yourself, but I have an idea. Even though he doesn't know what you look like for certain, I'm sure if he snooped around in New York City, someone had to give him a description of you."

Jack shook his head. "He'd pick me right out of the crowd then."

Marlene stood, the sheet falling to the floor. "Not if you're incognito."

"How am I supposed to think, Marlene. You've absolutely distracted me again."

She walked towards her husband. "Don't think, Jack. We've got some time before the funeral."

<> <>

After Grant Jennings heard what was going on, they decided to skip church and keep Charlotte at the farm. He rode into town to let them know. Jack's farm house was quite busy that morning, with men coming and going. It was good the boarding house where the reporter stayed last night wasn't within distance. Still, Jack hoped the commotion didn't draw too much attention.

Along with Grant and a few other men who had stopped by, they explained the plans that were being made to drive an empty coffin through town while the townsfolk followed behind to the graveyard.

"Jack, we have to go to your funeral," Marlene told him. Her words sounded quite ridiculous. "They said to meet at the church at eleven."

"It's pretty dangerous to do so. He may recognize me."

Marlene laughed, a sly smile covering her face. Jack wasn't sure what she had planned. "He will never recognize you, Aunt Josephine."

Grant, Noah, Sheriff Nightingale and a few other men roared with laughter.

"Over my dead body! I ain't dressing up like no woman!"

"Come on, don't be a spoiled sport! Why hide here and miss all the action."

"I ain't putting on a dress. No way!" Jack didn't mind being teased but his wife was having way too much fun with this. He did enjoy watching her smile and laugh. Marlene had finally come out of her shell. He'd like to think he had something to do with the end results.

"I'm teasing, Jack! I have something else in mind. The man who sold you this house left a trunk full of clothing. I noticed it before. Why don't we take a look and you can be Uncle Joe instead?"

"That's better. Ok, I'm all for having a bit of fun." He turned to the men, who tried to hide their smirks. "This won't ever be mentioned outside of this house."

The men mumbled how they'd never tell a soul but when they left, their laughter resonated up his walkway and back in the house.

Jack rubbed his chin. He'd probably never hear the end of his wife wanting to dress him up like some old woman!

"Come along, Jack. We have some work to do."

<><>

"Shh. You have to lower your voice. Make it sound old and tired."

"I'm not old and tired. This is insane. I'm going home."

Marlene nudged him with her elbow. Then she raised her voice. "Now, now, Uncle Joe. I know you loved him. Please, stop crying."

"I'm not crying," he told her, frustrated. She thought this was so funny. Well, he had to admit, his wife was quite the kidder.

Jack wore a pair of black brushed cotton trousers, along with a white dress shirt with a high collar and a pure black silk puff tie. His hands were covered with a pair of black deerskin dress gloves and he wore a striped Galloway vest over the shirt. To top off his fancy wear, he hung a black rifle frock coat over his shoulders. He leaned in, whispering in Marlene's ear. "This flour is starting to get itchy. I want to take this hat off and scratch my head."

"You can't. Be brave, Jack. Aren't you having fun?"

He grinned. "Maybe a little." He had to admit, it took them longer than they had planned to get ready for the service. Marlene had decided to put flour in his hair to give him an aged, greying look. He got a bright idea of doing the same to her and they wound up with a ton of flour on the floor and all over them. That's when Marlene decided to pretend she was his wife instead of his daughter. They both had greying hair and she wore dark stockings with a black dress, hiding her hair under a hat with netting. No one was able to see she was so young. She had even found a pair of black gloves to match her own outfit.

The two of them made quite the handsome couple. They walked out of the church, Jack leaning heavily on a cane while Marlene held onto him with a stooped back. They got in line behind the others and noticed the reporter was one row ahead of them, taking notes as he walked. He pushed his glasses up his nose several times when they almost fell off.

As the procession began, music from a guitar and fiddle rent the air. Jack stretched his neck to see a red-headed cowboy leading the way, playing a slow ballad on his fiddle while the young man beside him strummed a slow tune on his guitar.

Someone yelled out, "Rusty, that old coot still plays the fiddle like nobody's business."

The crowd murmured until several of the ladies tried to shush everyone.

"This is a funeral, folks, keep it down in front," the reverend stated.

Jack whispered in Marlene's ear. "Watch that reporter as he is sticking his neck out to see what's going on. Notice Sam Smith from the livery moves right in front of him so he can't see."

"So does Dr. Hart and his wife. They are walking along side of him. Every time he moves to look, the doctor gets in his way."

Jack grinned. Everyone sure was going out of their way to make sure J. Fergy did rest in peace. Even Mr. Beadle was here, walking in the front of the crowd. He hung his head as if he lost his best friend. He walked with the Young and White families, who all showed up after getting word from one of their cow hands who had been in town for the wedding what happened. They lived twenty minutes away and made a point of being here to support Jack today. He shook his head. These people were truly amazing.

Jack lifted his head and prayed to God above this would work. Once J. Fergy was laid to rest, he'd start over, closing the door to the past and begin a new phase of his writing career.

The voices of many of the townsfolk blended in harmony as they belted out;

Shall we meet beyond the river,
In the clime where angels dwell?
Shall we meet where friendship never
Saddest tales of sorrow tell?
Shall we meet our loved companions,
On that brighter, fairer shore,
When this life's great work is ended,
Shall we meet to part no more?
Yes, we'll meet beyond the river,
Where our joys shall never die,
We shall meet our loved and saved ones,
In that happy by and by.

Jack clasped Marlene's hand and stood with the crowd as they lowered J. Fergy's coffin in the ground. "I almost feel as if I'm saying goodbye to a friend," Jack told her.

She held on tighter. "You are."

Perhaps she was right. It was time to lay the name to rest. I had brought him great joy when he was building a career and made him tons of money. It also caused him so much grief, losing his sister, his parents love. J. Fergy almost caused him to become a broken man. Until he met Marlene.

Today was a new start. A future. A second chance.

Chapter 10

3 months later

Charlotte squirmed. "Now, hold still, child. I'm not going to hurt you!" Frustrated, Marlene tried to finish the child's hair. "All done. I see Uncle Mack coming up the walk."

"Goodbye Mommie! Daddy!" She gave each parent a hug and kiss and ran out the door with her lunch pail.

"He still comes for her, every morning like clockwork," Jack mumbled. He was opening a package that had arrived this morning.

Marlene refilled their coffee and sat down at the table with him. "Mack enjoys picking her up and taking her to school. Besides, he says he has to check on his wife, make sure she is feeling well."

Jack grinned. "I see him over at the school more than at the sheriff's office. For a deputy, he sure doesn't go by the rules."

Marlene laughed. "I doubt Sheriff Nightingale is worried. He's happy to have Mack working with him. Besides, Mack doesn't have to work. The reward money he received for finding those railroad certificates is more than enough where they can live in comfort. Mack's problem is he can't be idle."

"Seems like they have been pretty busy from the announcement they made last week. It's only been three months since the wedding."

Marlene shook her head. "Oh, Jack. It doesn't take long to conceive a baby."

Jack agreed. "I guess you're right. We need to work on that some more."

Marlene smiled. "We have been, husband. Every day and night."

He gave her a cheeky grin. "Don't hurt to try some more."

"Husband, you are too frisky."

He leaned over the table to kiss her. "You make me that way."

She kissed him back and pointed to the package. "What do you have there?"

"My new life."

Marlene set her cup down. "May I see, please?"

"For a kiss."

"How about two, one now and one before you start working?"

"Deal." He handed the book to her.

Marlene ran her fingers over the yellow-toned cover. The words stood out in bold black ink. "*Tales in a Texas Town or The Mysterious Adventures of Charlie and Clarissa.*" The cover had a photo of a cow that looked pretty close to Clarissa and a young boy. She looked at her husband with a new respect.

"What do you think?"

"I think it's wonderful."

"I wanted to add Charlotte's name but my publisher insisted the hero had to be a boy, hence, Charlie, since mostly young boys will read this. Somehow I'm going to write Charlotte into a scene or two. Maybe she will be the annoying but sweet little sister."

She noticed right away his legal name as that of the writer. Surprised, she looked at her husband. "You did not use a fictitious name."

He shook his head then looked at her. Jack crossed his arms over his chest. "When Beadle was here he told me that when they investigated the murder they found out my sister had been communicating with the stalker's brother. It had more to do with her than me. This woman knew she was there and broke in. I guess my fame made it easier to find my sister. She saw my sister as a threat somehow in her deranged mind. It wasn't just because of my books. There was more to it than they told us because they wanted to spare my parents."

"I'm sorry, Jack. You've carried the burden of her death for so long."

"I still feel responsible. Because I did book signings as J. Fergy and was in the public eye more so than not, it wasn't hard to follow me home and find out where I lived."

She got up and wrapped her arms around his shoulders, standing behind him. "You must stop blaming yourself. It's not your fault."

"I'm learning, Marlene. Only time will heal these feelings. It's why I decided I'm not hiding my name any longer. In order to move on I'm declaring Jack Fergenson is the proud author of these new dime novels. I'm also going to be writing a story once a month for the Wichita Falls newspaper."

Marlene hugged him. "Good for you. The whole town will be proud to know you."

"As long as there are no crazed fans."

"Or, a nosey newspaper reporter. That one sure left town in a hurry the other week after J. Fergy's funeral."

Jack laughed. "Well, he was asking questions even after the funeral so he could do a write up on the last days of J. Fergy's life. The sheriff was getting tired of him and noticed that busy-body Miss Steele from the Teacher's Association was back in town. So, he sicked her on him. In a matter of less than an hour, the reporter left, the dust from his buggy clouding the streets."

Marlene got a good laugh at that story. "I'm sure he got all he needed from her. I hope she doesn't bother Jennie too much. That woman is a shrew! She won't stop harassing poor Jennie."

"I think Jennie can handle her. As a matter of fact, I'm starting to wander if Miss Steele comes back for the teacher at all. I've seen her eyeing up one of our townsfolk."

"Oh? Mister Fergenson, what in the world are you watching Miss Steele for?"

"Now, darling, this was before you and I were together. I observe people, it's what I do as a writer."

"Hmm, that sounds a bit fishy to me." She loved teasing her husband. "If you know so much, who is she eyeing up?"

Jack stood up and threw the book on the table. He picked his wife up and began to carry her upstairs. "You will have to force it out of me, Mrs. Fergenson."

Marlene giggled and held on. "I certainly will, sir."

<> <>

A week later Charlotte had just left for school with Mack when a buggy stopped in front of the boarding house. Marlene was on her way to see Doc Hart when she noticed an older couple disembark. They looked around as if lost.

The woman was tiny but she wore a black dress and veil. It was hard to see her face. Marlene gasped when the man turned to stare at her. He was an older version of Jack, his hair gray, almost white. She knew right away it was Jack's parents, he had the same hazel eyes as his son. She wanted to rush home and tell him but wanted to make sure it was them. "Hello, may I help you find someone?"

"We are looking for the grave site of J. Fergy. Can you direct us to the cemetery?"

Marlene wanted to tell them their son was not dead. She had to make sure. "Are you friends of the great writer?"

"No. We're family. Now, can you tell us where we may find it?"

"Yes, sir. Straight out of town and bear to the right. You'll see it over the small hump. "

"Thank you, miss." The woman nodded and allowed her husband to help her back in the buggy.

Marlene watched as they made their way to the edge of town. She lifted her skirts and flew down the road towards home. Flinging the gate open, she ran up the two steps, calling for Jack. "Hurry, Jack, come down here!"

"What is it?"

She didn't mean to put the ferocious look on his face when he raced down from the upstairs.

"You have some visitors!" She was trying to speak while catching her breath.

"Where? I don't see anyone." Jack peeked out the door, then turned back to look at her leaning against the wall.

"Not here, Jack. Oh my! It's your parents."

Jack stilled. "What!"

"They asked for directions to the cemetery."

"They think I'm dead. Dear Lord, I didn't send them a letter telling them what we did, although I didn't think it was necessary since they haven't spoken to me since my sister's death."

Marlene had a hold of herself. She pushed from the wall. "We've been too busy to realize they knew your pen name. I'm so sorry, Jack. Go on, go make things right."

Jack hesitated. He tried to hide a flash of anger that crossed his face. She reached up to hold his cheeks in her hands. "Forgiveness will set you free, Jack. You may have hard feelings about what happened. I'm sure you are hurt but not forgiving them will break your heart, Jack. You can't be a good parent unless you treat your own well."

Jack hung his head. "How did you know I was feeling spiteful? My first thought was to let them believe I'm dead, too. When my sister died, they refused to speak to me. I was hurting, blaming myself and it didn't help they blamed me as well."

"Time heals."

"You know it better than anyone, Marlene. It's why I love you."

She gave him a sweet kiss and pushed him out the door. "No, go on. You know what to do."

She watched him hurry through town, his long strides taking him towards the edge of town where the cemetery and his parents were. Then he stopped, turned and began racing through the street as fast as he could. Marlene went outside, down the walk and began to walk towards him. What in the world?

When he reached her, he bent over, hands on his knees, breathing erratically. Once he caught his breath he took hold of her shoulders and gave her a long, deep kiss in the middle of the street. Shocked, she looked at him with eyes wide. "Jack, what in the world?"

"It hit me as I'm walking along to the cemetery, Marlene. You said I can't be a good parent unless I treat mine well. Does that mean what I think it does?"

She nodded, not realizing she had said those words earlier. "I wanted to confirm it with Doc Hart first before I told you for sure."

"Is that where you were going this morning?"

"Sure was and I am late so I've got to go, Jack. Go on, now."

"I'll drop you off."

"If you insist." She ran inside to get her reticule. Her husband stood in the middle of the street, patiently waiting on her. When she met up with him, he wrapped an arm around her and delivered her to the doctor's office.

"I'll be back shortly. I don't want you to leave here until I can walk you home."

"Jack, that's overbearing. I can walk home myself."

He shook his head. "It's too dangerous."

Marlene placed a hand on her hip. "Dangerous? Jack, that's ridiculous!"

"Please, Marlene. I have to deal with my parents right now. I'd feel better if you waited for me."

"Why didn't you say so. I'll be inside or on the bench outside if there is room," she told him. "Now get moving. You've stalled enough."

He took off down the street while she went to her appointment. After the doc confirmed she was indeed with child, Marlene let the tears run across her cheeks unchecked. When she left the office, the bench outside was filled with other patients so Marlene made her way down the street towards the edge of town. She was filled with so much joy she didn't think to wait there.

All she wanted was to tell Jack and have him hold her in his arms. Hurrying past the saloon, she crossed the street at the edge of town. The buggy had stopped at the cemetery and the three of them stood there, looking down at the grave.

Then Jack's mother turned and took her son in her arms and Jack's father followed. Marlene felt like an intruder until Jack looked up to see her standing there. He motioned for her to come closer. "This is my wife."

Jack's father grinned. "We've already met, I believe," he said before putting an arm out to include her in their circle of hugs.

Mrs. Fergenson took her hand. "Welcome to our family."

"Thank you. Why don't we go to the house and have something to eat. I'm sure you must be starved by now."

"How about if we treat the both of you to lunch at the small restaurant we noticed as we came through town."

"How about the three of us?" Marlene heard Jack's intake of breath.

"Marlene," he said, his raspy voice close to her ear. "Are we? Is it?"

She nodded. "For sure, Jack. Congratulations, you are going to be a father."

He wrapped his arms around her and gave her a kiss so sweet Marlene wanted to cry.

A cough interrupted the two.

Jack moved away. "I'm sorry, Mother, I got carried away. But you'll be happy to know you are going to be a grandmother!"

A tear fell from his mother's cheek. Mr. Fergenson took his handkerchief and wiped it away. "Come along, everyone. Now we have something else to celebrate." After dropping the buggy at the livery, they walked to the restaurant together.

Boy what a celebration. Before they were finished with their meal, the rest of the patrons found out about the baby because Jack told every soul who entered through the front door. His dad thought Jack was going overboard but Jack didn't care. He wanted to shout it to the world.

"Father, will you stay awhile? We have plenty of room for the both of you?"

"A week at the most, son. I have a big case coming up in a few weeks."

"My father is one of the best district attorney's on the east coast, Marlene. He's helped to put away some bad people."

"I'm impressed, sir. Then you will be a fine grandfather. We'll tell stories of your mighty deeds."

His father grinned.

His mother rolled her eyes.

Jack had a smile on his face a mile wide.

Marlene sighed. Then she realized the whole town knew about her baby except for her own baby. Charlotte! "Oh, dear! Jack, I haven't told Charlotte about the baby. I don't want her to hear it from anyone else."

Jack stood. "We have to go."

Jack's parents followed them across the street to the school house. Marlene went inside while they all waited in the yard. She told Jennie what happened so the child was able to leave. Pretty soon, she had a curious Charlotte running down the steps and jumping into Jack's arms.

"Hello, princess. I have some wonderful news."

Charlotte placed her little hands on his cheeks and looked him right in the eye. "You do?"

"Yes, I want you to meet your grandparents."

"I have grandparents? Mommie, what are grandparents?"

Before Marlene was able to answer, she slid down from Jack and stood in front of his mother. "Hello, are you my grandparents?"

Mrs. Fergenson, who had pulled back her veil since she really wasn't mourning anyone any longer, smiled. She held out a gloved hand. "Yes. How do you do?"

Charlotte took her hand and shook it. "I'm Charlotte. Do you want to go to the farm on Saturday to see Clarissa? She's my cow. I have friends there, too. You can come with if you promise to eat all your vegetables."

Jack's mother laughed along with the others. "I believe we can arrange to tag along with you. We are going to stay for a week."

Charlotte's eyes got huge. "A whole week!" She turned to Marlene. "Mommie, can I stay home from school to spend time with my new grandparents?"

"I think we'll take today off but you have to go to school tomorrow." Before Charlotte began to whine, she added, " How about we talk about it later? I have some other good news to tell you about when we get home."

"Okay."

Charlotte looked up at her new grandparents and took each of their hands as they all walked back home.

Jack and Marlene followed behind, their arms around each other.

"I love you, Marlene."

"Oh, Jack. I love you more."

He shook his head. "There's no way. You can't possibly love me more than what I'm feeling right now, this very moment."

"Oh, I bet I can show you," she teased.

He nuzzled her ear. "Come to think of it, I bet you can."

"That's right, Jack. Don't you ever forget it."

"I never will, my darling."

Marlene looked up to see her brother watching from the sheriff's front porch. She waved to him, then looked up to the sky, thanking God he found her that day.

She'd come a long way since then, thanks to Jack Fergenson and a cow named Clarissa.

****

Thanks for reading Jack and Marlene's story.
Have you read the other stories in the Brides of Mill Ridge series?
You can read the whole series in one shot with the box set.
Get Brides of Mill Ridge box set available on Amazon![1]
(https://www.amazon.com/gp/product/B07NKCHCTB)

*****

I wonder who Miss Steele was paying attention to in Mill Ridge? She's been a miserable pain in the side to Miss Jennie, the school teacher, trying to oust her from her job. Her position in the Teacher's Association makes her hated by most. Why in the world would anyone take an interest in her?
You can read Miss Steele's story in CHRISTMAS IN MILL RIDGE, a special story just for my readers.
GET [2]CHIRSTMAS[3] IN MILL RIDGE[4]
(https://www.amazon.com/Christmas-Mill-Ridge-Brides-Book-ebook/dp/B08HR9P48B/)
NOW AVAILABLE ON AMAZON![5] (https://www.amazon.com/Christmas-Mill-Ridge-Brides-Book-ebook/dp/B08HR9P48B/)

---

1. https://www.amazon.com/gp/product/B07NKCHCTB

2. https://www.amazon.com/Christmas-Mill-Ridge-Brides-Book-ebook/dp/B08HR9P48B/

3. https://www.amazon.com/Christmas-Mill-Ridge-Brides-Book-ebook/dp/B08HR9P48B/

4. https://www.amazon.com/Christmas-Mill-Ridge-Brides-Book-ebook/dp/B08HR9P48B/

5. https://www.amazon.com/Christmas-Mill-Ridge-Brides-Book-ebook/dp/B08HR9P48B/